Geronimo Stilton

BACK IN TIME

THE SECOND JOURNEY THROUGH TIME

Scholastic Inc.

ISBN 978-0-545-74618-2

Based on an original idea by Elisabetta Dami.

www.geronimostilton.com

Published by Scholastic Inc., 557 Broadway, New York, NY 10012.

Text by Geronimo Stilton
Original title *Viaggio nel tempo-2*
Cover by Silvia Fusetti
Illustrations by Danilo Barozzi, Silvia Bigolin, Giorgio Campioni, Daria Cerchi, Sergio Favret, Giuseppe Ferrario, Umberta Pezzoli, Sabrina Stefanini, and Piemme's archives. 3-D backgrounds by Davide Turotti.
Coloring by Christian Aliprandi.
Graphics by Merenguita Gingermousee, Yuko Egusa, and Sara Baruffaldi.

Special thanks to Shannon Penney
Translated by Julia Heim
Interior design by Kay Petronio

12 11 10 9 8 7 6 5 4 3 2 1   15 16 17 18 19/0

Printed in Singapore   46

First printing, February 2015

VOYAGERS ON THE SECOND JOURNEY THROUGH TIME

Dear rodent friends,
My name is Stilton, *Geronimo Stilton*. I am the editor and publisher of *The Rodent's Gazette*, the most famouse newspaper on Mouse Island. I'm about to tell you the story of one of my most incredible adventures! But first, let me introduce the other mice in this story . . .

THEA STILTON
My sister, Thea, is athletic and brave! She's also a special correspondent for *The Rodent's Gazette*.

BENJAMIN
Benjamin is my favorite little nephew. He's a sweet and caring mouselet, and he makes me so proud!

TRAP
My cousin Trap is a terrible prankster sometimes! His favorite hobby is playing jokes on me . . . but he's family, and I love him!

PROFESSOR PAWS VON VOLT
Professor von Volt is a genius inventor who has dedicated his life to making amazing new discoveries. His latest invention is the Rodent Relocator, a new kind of time machine!

A NIGHT JUST LIKE
ANY OTHER . . .
OR WAS IT?

It started out as a regular night, just like any other.
It was a **cold** Friday in autumn, and I had
stayed late at the office. I'm a very *busy* mouse!

This is me,
Geronimo
Stilton, in
my office!

Oops, I'm sorry — I haven't introduced myself! My name is Stilton, *Geronimo Stilton*. I run *The Rodent's Gazette*, the most famouse newspaper on Mouse Island.

As I was saying, I got home very late that night, around **MIDNIGHT**. I was too tired to squeak! I couldn't wait to go to **bed**.

But first, I put on my pajamas and flopped in an armchair in front of the fireplace to relax with some **chocolate Cheesy Chews**. Just then . . .

Professor von Volt's alarm!

. . . a ten-thousand-**megawatt** alarm pierced my ears! Holey cheese, I'd know that sound anywhere! It was the **alarm** that Professor von Volt had installed in my house. It only rang when he needed my help right away!

My whiskers **trembled**. What could be wrong?

I jumped to my paws, but as I did, *I HIT MY HEAD ON A SHELF*! I was completely **dazed**. As I stumbled around, I walked into a lamp, snoutfirst!

Then I slipped on a chocolate Cheesy Chew, fell backward near the fireplace, and **scorched** my tail! Rats!

I jumped up again, yelping, **"Ahhhhhh!"**

I was so panicked that I banged into a little table — and knocked over my beloved **red fish**, Hannibal's,

1 Yum!

I was calmly munching on a piece of chocolate near the fireplace, when . . .

2 ???

. . . a ten-thousand-megawatt alarm pierced my ears . . .

3 Bonk!

. . . I jumped up and hit my head on a shelf . . .

4 Huh?

. . . I was completely dazed . . .

5 Oof!

. . . I walked into a lamp, snoutfirst . . .

6 Aaaahh!

. . . I slipped on a chocolate Cheesy Chew and fell backward . . .

7

. . . I landed near the fireplace and scorched my tail . . .

8

. . . I banged into a small table and knocked over the fishbowl . . .

9

. . . which belonged to my beloved little red fish, Hannibal . . .

10

. . . so I scooped him up and ran to the bathroom . . .

11

. . . I refilled the fishbowl, and he began swimming again . . .

12

. . . and finally, I breathed a sigh of relief. Hannibal was okay. Whew!

fishbowl! I scooped him up and ran to the bathroom to refill the fishbowl with water. Thankfully, poor Hannibal was okay. **WHEW!**

Once I had a moment to catch my breath, I remembered something . . .

This had all started with Professor von Volt's **alarm**. He needed my help!

I looked out the window and saw an extremely **loooong** camper driving down the road. It sparkled like a mirror.

Huh? Thundering cat tails — that camper was **Professor von Volt's secret laboratory**!

I changed out of my pajamas in two shakes of a mouse's tail, and headed outside to find the professor.

A SUPER-SECRET SECRET!

Have you met **PROFESSOR VON VOLT** before?

In case you haven't, let me tell you, the professor is the smartest mouse I know! I first met him a long time ago. In fact, he was the one who took

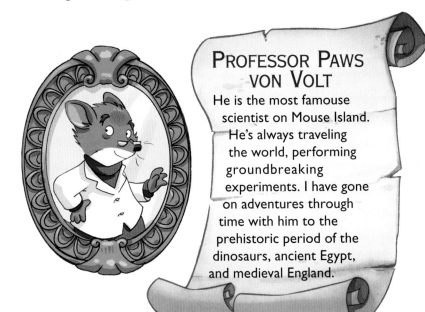

PROFESSOR PAWS VON VOLT

He is the most famouse scientist on Mouse Island. He's always traveling the world, performing groundbreaking experiments. I have gone on adventures through time with him to the prehistoric period of the dinosaurs, ancient Egypt, and medieval England.

me on my very first JOURNEY THROUGH TIME...

PROFESSOR VON VOLT carries out his experiments in secret locations so that no other mice can SPY on him.

His inventions must remain top secret! That's why NO ONE ever knows where he is. The professor once told me that I'm the only one he trusts, because I am a true gentlemouse!

The professor works in a laboratory inside a large camper that sparkles like a mirror. He travels around and NEVER stays in one place for too long.

I'll give you a sneak peek into his laboratory. But shhh — it's a SUPER-SECRET secret. Don't tell anyone!

I'll give you a sneak peek!

THE SECRET LABORATORY

ENTRANCE

FIRST SECTION

# of Professor von Volt!

SOLAR PANELS

MYSTERIOUS OBJECT

TURN THE PAGE TO SEE THE OTHER PARTS OF THE CAMPER!

SOLAR PANELS

ARCHIVES

BRAINSTORMING ROOM

VAULT

MUSIC ROOM

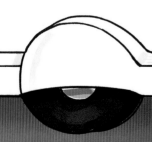

LIBRARY

SECOND SECTION

COMPUTER LAB

DATA-PROCESSING CENTER

SCIENCE LAB

TURN THE PAGE TO SEE THE LAST PART OF THE CAMPER!

BEDROOM

WATER RESERVES

H₂O

BATHROOM

KITCHEN

PANTRY

THIRD SECTION

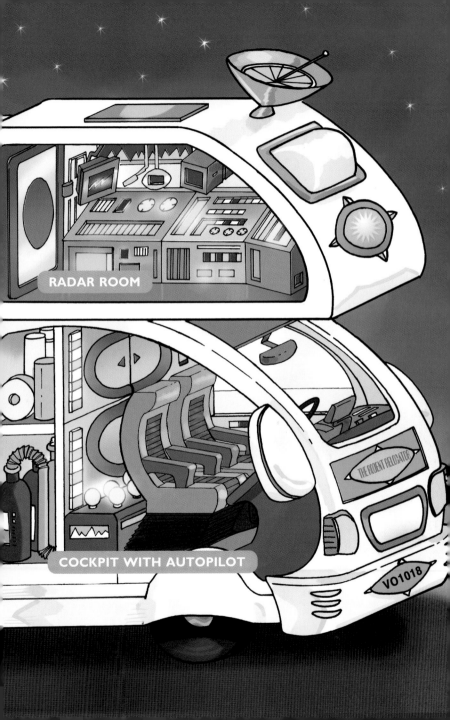

RADAR ROOM

COCKPIT WITH AUTOPILOT

THE RODENT RELOCATOR

VO1018

STILTOON, GERONIMO STILTOON!

I ran up behind the camper and yelled, "Professor von Volt! It's me, *Geronimo Stilton*! Stop!" The camper screeched to a halt, and I took a closer look at the outside.

The body looked like a MIRROR, the fenders looked like MIRRORS, the hubcaps looked like MIRRORS, the lights looked like MIRRORS . . . even the windows looked like MIRRORS!

It was impossible to tell what was inside — even though I knew! A rolling shutter lifted on the back of the camper and a metallic voice crackled, "Come in!"

I stepped inside, and the camper immediately took off down the street.

WHEW! JUST IN TIME!

The automatic door shut behind me with a quiet hissing sound. **Ppffffff!**

I was standing in front of a **MYSTERIOUS** object covered with a black cloth. Cheese niblets, what could it be?

Before I could investigate, a ten-thousand-watt light **blinded** me! A video camera popped up,

(1)

(2)

RECORDING my every move.

A metallic voice crackled, *"STAY STILL, PLEASE!"* (1)

I whirled around, shocked.

The voice repeated, *"I SAID STAY STILL, PLEASE!"* Then it added, *"WHISKER EXTRACTION FOR IDENTIFICATION!"* (2)

Before I **KNEW** what was happening, a pair of tweezers had **SWOOPED** out of nowhere and yanked out one of my whiskers!

"Ooouuch!" I squeaked.

A microscope began to examine my whisker.

Whisker for identification

BZZZ . . . (3)

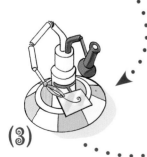

(3)

A moment later, my snout appeared up on a screen! (4)

The crackly voice said, *"WHISKER IDENTIFIED! IT BELONGS TO A RODENT BY THE NAME OF STILTOON, GERONIMO STILTOON!"*

I sighed and corrected it. "My name is Stilton, *Geronimo Stilton*!"

GERONIMO STILTOON

(4)

THE RODENT
RELOCATOR

Just then, a door burst open and a snout that I knew appeared.

"PROFESSOR VON VOLT!" I squeaked happily. It was wonderful to see my old friend.

He gave me a hug. "Geronimo Stilton! What can I do for you?"

Moldy mozzarella, what did he mean? "But, Professor, you're the one who called me with your ALARM!" I said.

The professor scratched his whiskers. "Huh? Oh yes, now I remember! I had to tell you something IMPORTANT. But what was it? Hmm . . ." Then he smacked his forehead with his paw. "Oh, putrid cheese puffs, it's midnight! I didn't realize it was so late. I'm sorry, Geronimo!

I am such a distracted mouse . . ."

I smiled. "It doesn't matter that it's late. You can call me any time, day or NiGHT!"

"Do you remember our first JOURNEY THROUGH TIME?" the professor asked me.

I couldn't help sighing **happily**. I may have even gotten a little misty-eyed. (I'm a very Sentimental mouse.) "How could I forget the most amazing and fascinating experience of my life, Professor?"

Ta-da!

He patted my paw. "Stay calm, Geronimo — I have a SURPRISE for you. This is my brand-new invention . . ."

The professor announced, "I call it . . . THE RODENT RELOCATOR!"

A big, spherical machine with a shiny surface!

My jaw hung open, and my whiskers trembled with excitement. Before me was a big, spherical machine with a shiny surface. I could hardly squeak!

Volt smiled at my reaction. "It's my new TIME-TRAVEL machine! It is much, much, much more advanced than the Mouse Mover 3000, which we used on our last adventure. Now let me explain how it works — but when I'm done, remind me that I have to tell you something else that is very, very important. I'm very easily distracted, after all!"

THE RODENT RELOCATOR

NAME: The Rodent Relocator
SPEED: Three times faster than the speed of light
SEATS: Four grown mice
MATERIAL: Made of super-lightweight titanium
MEASUREMENTS: Fit for a mouse

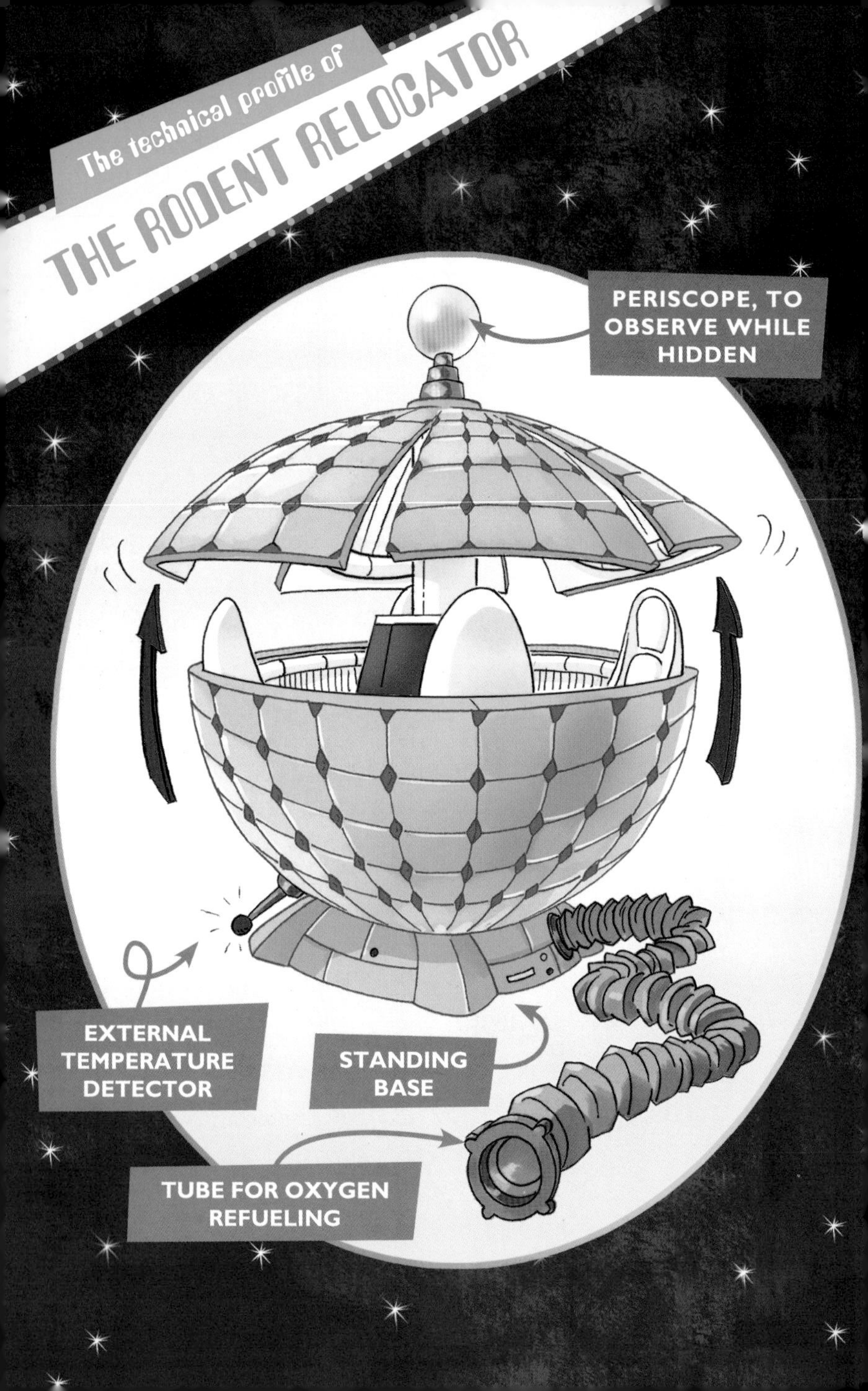

The technical profile of
THE RODENT RELOCATOR
PERISCOPE, TO OBSERVE WHILE HIDDEN
EXTERNAL TEMPERATURE DETECTOR
STANDING BASE
TUBE FOR OXYGEN REFUELING

PERISCOPE REENTRY

PERISCOPE EXTENSION

JETS BENEATH THE STANDING BASE

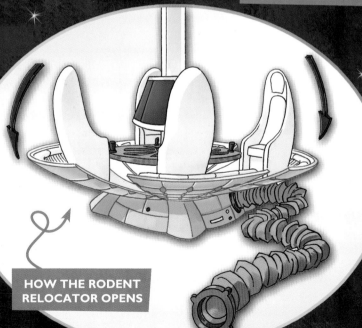

BEFORE DEPARTURE, THE OXYGEN TUBE MUST RETRACT

HOW THE RODENT RELOCATOR OPENS

EACH SEAT IS EQUIPPED WITH SAFETY BELTS

THERMAL SUITS FOR THE CREW

RED BUTTON!

THE MYSTERIOUS
MICRO MOUSE!

PROFESSOR VON VOLT whispered, "That's not all. I invented something else incredible."

Intrigued, I asked, "What?"

"It's called the MICRO MOUSE!" he said in a hushed voice.

"MICRO MOUSE?" I repeated. "Professor, why are we whispering?"

He looked around nervously. "I know it seems silly, Geronimo, but I'm always afraid that someone is spying on me. There are many dishonest rodents out there. They could be interested in my inventions, so I have to be very careful!"

With that, the professor opened his safe and pulled out a STRANGE object.

He strapped it onto his wrist, satisfied. "Let me

introduce you to the **Micro Mouse**: a very
powerful but very small and lightweight
computer. It's so small that a mouse can
wear it on his wrist! There's only one,
and it's for you to wear, Geronimo."

Rat-munching rattlesnakes!
Did he mean what I **thought** he meant?

But before I could squeak, the professor went
on. "It provides **information** about historic time
periods and allows you to surf the web, take
pictures, and record video. It works as a cell phone,
a television, and a satellite navigation system so
that you can orient yourself
in the past. It runs on **solar**
and **wind energy**, so it's even
good for the environment. If
you push a special button,
it also becomes invisible!
Here's how it works . . ."

Here's the
Micro Mouse!

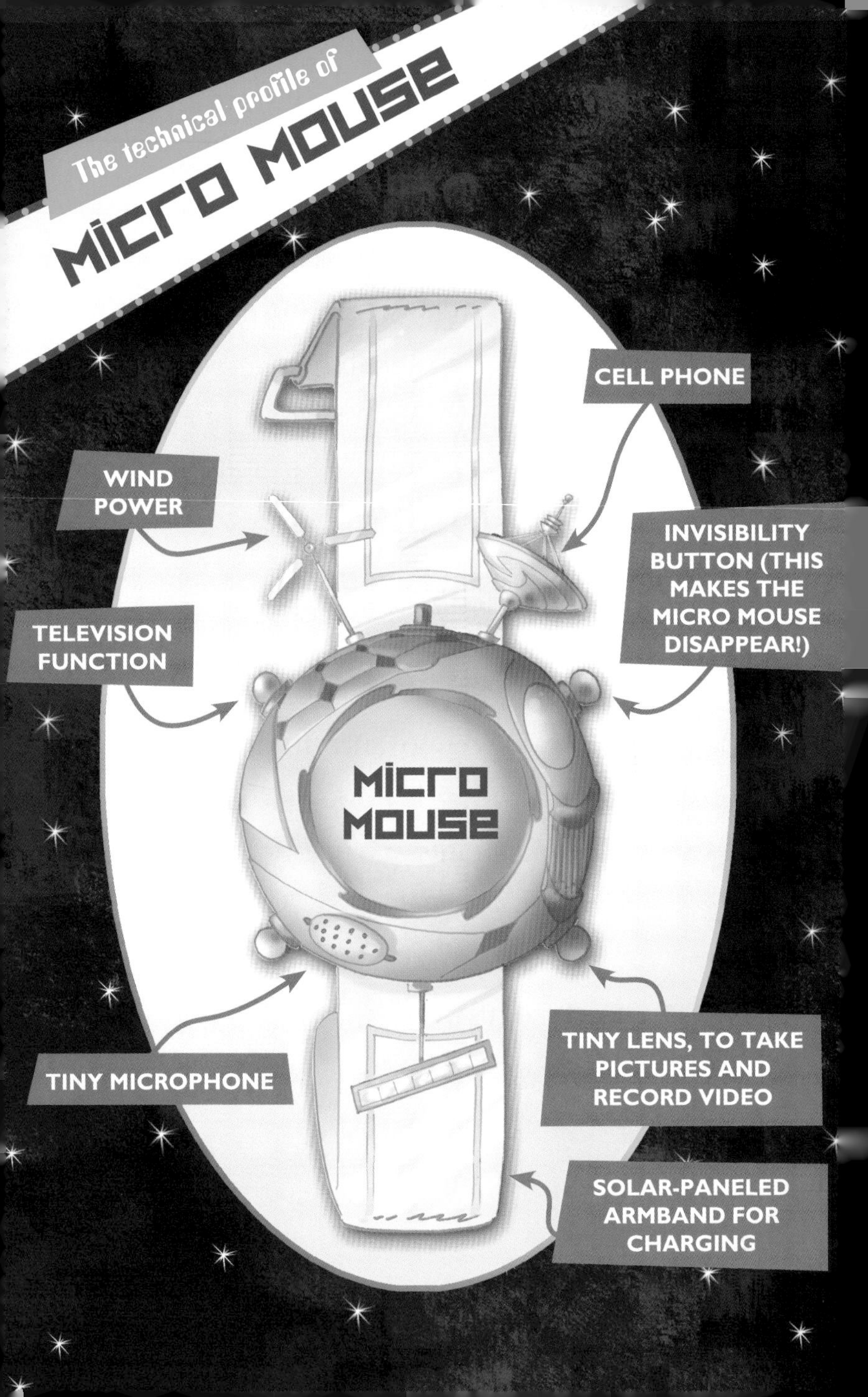
The technical profile of
MICRO MOUSE
CELL PHONE
WIND POWER
INVISIBILITY BUTTON (THIS MAKES THE MICRO MOUSE DISAPPEAR!)
TELEVISION FUNCTION
MICRO MOUSE
TINY MICROPHONE
TINY LENS, TO TAKE PICTURES AND RECORD VIDEO
SOLAR-PANELED ARMBAND FOR CHARGING

USEFUL INFORMATION

DATE AND
DESTINATION
SETTINGS

SATELLITE NAVIGATION
SYSTEM, TO ORIENT
YOURSELF WHEN
TRAVELING TO THE PAST

IT'S NICE TO DREAM, BUT IT'S BETTER TO LIVE YOUR DREAMS!

Finally, I was able to get a squeak in. "So are we leaving for a new JOURNEY THROUGH TIME, Professor?" I asked, my tail twitching with excitement. "Where will we go this time?"

He raised an eyebrow. "It's not where *we* are going, Geronimo, but where *you* are going! This time you will travel alone. I'm still an **adventurous** mouse at heart, but I am too old to handle the HEAT of the jungle, climb any **ancient** walls, or taste the STRANGE foods of faraway lands."

Rancid ricotta, I had to go **ALONE**?!

The professor must have sensed my panic, because he smiled. "It will be just like I'm there, too," he said. "Now, here's where I'm sending you."

Professor von Volt during our first journey through time — in the extremely humid forest of the prehistoric period of the dinosaurs!

He announced, "First, you will go to **ancient Rome** in 45 BCE!"

My snout lit up. "Ancient Rome? That sounds fabumouse!"

Volt continued, "Then you'll visit the **Maya civilization** in 1005 CE!"

I was so **excited**, I could barely squeak. "I've always dreamed of uncovering the secrets of the Maya people. I can't wait!"

The professor **chuckled**. "Patience, Geronimo! I haven't even told you about your final stop: **Versailles, France**, in 1682 CE, the age of King Louis XIV — the Sun King!"

I did a happy dance on the spot. "That's one of the most fascinating historical periods of all!" I cried.

Suddenly, Volt turned serious. "Geronimo, it will be a **wonderful** journey, and I hope it will give you material to write a really mouserific new book. But there is always a small possibility that you will **get lost** in time and be stuck in the past forever. Are you still up for it?"

My fur stood on end. I thought it over. The most important thing I had learned from my adventures was that it's nice to **dream**, but it's better to live your dreams — even if it takes courage! It also often takes the help of friends and family — plus, adventures are even more **Fabumouse** when shared with others!

So I nodded firmly. "Professor, I accept! But on one condition: Can I bring my **family** with me?"

I thought back on my first journey through time...

"Of course!" the professor agreed. I thought back on my first JOURNEY THROUGH TIME . . .

GERONIMO'S FIRST JOURNEY THROUGH TIME!

During my first journey through time, aboard the Mouse Mover 3000, there were five of us: Professor von Volt and four members of the Stilton family — me, Thea, Trap, and Benjamin!

In the time of the dinosaurs!

What a mouserific adventure!

In ancient Egypt!

In medieval England!

We went back to the prehistoric period of the dinosaurs, then to ancient Egypt, and finally to King Arthur's time, in medieval England. Then we returned to New Mouse City, but . . .

At the end of our adventure, my cousin Trap accidentally started the Mouse Mover 3000 again! I was afraid we'd be traveling through time forever, but luckily, the motor shut off, and we stayed home. Thank goodmouse!

The Mouse Mover 3000

SHHH! THIS IS TOP SECRET!

When I finally left the camper, it was already dawn. I was one exhausted rodent! I had spent the whole night discussing details of my trip with the professor. But I was too excited to rest. Instead, I ran to *The Rodent's Gazette* office and called my sister, THEA, my cousin Trap, and my nephew BENJAMIN right away.

Once we were all gathered in my office, I closed and **LOCKED** the door.

I told my assistant that I wasn't taking any calls.

And just to be SAFE, I even made sure that no one was spying through the window!

Then I whispered, "I met with Professor von Volt."

"Why are you acting so weird, Germeister?" Trap yelled. "What's with all the SECRECY?"

I murmured, "Shhh — someone might hear you! We have a secret mission to complete. We're headed on a fabumouse new JOURNEY THROUGH TIME, with a new time machine and three new destinations."

Trap grabbed his phone. "Holey cheese!" he cried. "What rattastic news! I have to tell all my friends right away!"

I grabbed his phone and hissed, "Shhh! This is top secret!"

"**Top secret?** Pfffft!" Trap scoffed. "You wrote a whole book about our first journey through time!"

The book written by Geronimo Stilton after his first journey through time!

I sighed, exasperated. "Yes, Trap, but I wrote it after we came back, not before we left! No one can know that we're going!"

Thea was on my side. "No

one can know, not even the staff of *The Rodent's Gazette.*

No one!
No one!
No one!"

Just then, sweet Benjamin squeaked up. "Um, Uncle, I have a **PROBLEM** — I don't think I can go! Next week, I have to turn in a big research project on **ancient Rome**, and I haven't even started yet." He looked down at his paws sadly. "I really don't know what to write! I'm not very good at **history**."

I put an arm around his shoulders. "Come with us! Traveling to the past will help you find information for your project. I'm hoping to find lots of material for my next book, too. We can **RESEARCH** together along the way — I bet you'll learn lots of things you didn't know!"

GOOD LUCK — BREAK A PAW!

With no time to waste, we headed to PROFESSOR VON VOLT'S camper. When we arrived, we all put on orange suits made especially for time travel.

Then we celebrated our departure with a bottle of whipped cheese and some Gorgonzola crackers. The professor proposed a toast. "To your trip into *hyperspace*!"

"Hyper-*what*?" Trap asked.

Hooray!

Congratulations!

Thanks!

Let's celebrate!

Squeak!

"We're used to space with three dimensions: height, **width**, and DEPTH," the professor explained. "Hyperspace can have four or five dimensions, maybe even more. *Isn't that incredible?*"

MOLDY MOZZARELLA! That sounded complicated.

"When you move through hyperspace, you can travel faster than the speed of LIGHT!" the professor added. "Until now, it's just been something you read about in science fiction. But I've figured out how to send **YOU** into hyperspace so you can travel through time!"

Trap giggled. "I'm hyper-happy to go into *hyperspace*! Should we have another **HYPER-NICE** toast? I'm **hyper-hungry**!"

The professor grinned. "Let me give you the instructions for this JOURNEY THROUGH TIME — and when I'm done, remind me to tell you why you should never touch the red button!"

Instructions for the
JOURNEY THROUGH TIME

1. HOW TO DEPART

The date, time, and place must be entered correctly on Geronimo's Micro Mouse. Be careful: BCE dates count backward: The year after 45 BCE is 44 BCE, then 43 BCE and so on. CE numbering becomes more normal: The year after I CE is 2 CE, then 3 CE and so on. After entering the date, press the OK button, and the Rodent Relocator will depart!

2. HOW TO RETURN

The date, time, and place must once again be entered into Geronimo's Micro Mouse. Then press the OK button, and the Rodent Relocator will bring you all back home. It's as simple as that!

3. HOW TO DRESS

In your bags, you will find appropriate clothing for ancient Rome, the Maya civilization, and the reign of the Sun King already packed for you.

4. HOW TO COMMUNICATE

Insert one of these tiny microphones inside your right ear. It will instantly translate what you hear, and allow you to speak in any language!

5. IF YOU GET LOST IN TIME?

Get comfortable — you're going to be there for a while!

while you're on your trip,

remember:

Never touch
the red
button!

We entered the Rodent Relocator, sat down, and buckled our seat belts.

The professor squeaked, "Are you ready to go? **Good luck**, my friends — *break a paw*!"

As the door closed, I remembered that the professor still hadn't told us **why** we should never touch the red button.

I yelled, "Professooooooooor!"

But it was too late. He couldn't hear us.

We were in complete **DARKNESS**.

I heard a buzz, and then the Rodent Relocator began to **VIBRATE**. It spun around faster and faster. I felt like I was being **crushed** into my seat! My head was spinning!

Ooooooooh, my head was *spinning and spinning and spinning and spinniiiing!*

46

THE RODENT RELOCATOR BEGAN TO SPIN AROUND FASTER AND FASTER AND FASTER AND FASTER AND FASTER AND FASTER AND FASTER AND FASTER AND FASTER AND FASTER . . .

Ugh, space sickness!

Chattering cheddar! My stomach was tied in knots, and I felt **super-queasy**!

Luckily, the professor had anticipated the space sickness. Beneath each of our seats were little motion sickness bags, just like on an airplane!

Finally, the **vibrations** died down. The **MICRO MOUSE** on my wrist announced: *"APPROACHING DESTINATION!"*

The Rodent Relocator stopped completely, and the Mirco Mouse announced, *"DESTINATION REACHED! WE ARE AT THE ROMAN FORUM, ON OCTOBER 10, 45 BCE!"*

MICRO MOUSE

ANCIENT
ROME

ANCIENT ROME

THE LEGEND OF ROMULUS AND REMUS

According to legend, twins Romulus and Remus were abandoned by their family and survived by drinking a wolf's milk as infants, until they were taken in by a shepherd. As adults, the twins decided to begin a town on the site where they had been saved. But they got into an argument — Romulus killed Remus, and then founded Rome, making himself the first king. He even named the city after himself!

THE BIRTH OF ROME

The exact date of Rome's founding is unknown, but the Romulus and Remus legend says that the city was founded in 753 BCE, and archaeological findings support that this date is possible. Originally, it was a small village on the banks of the Tiber River. Between the eighth and sixth centuries BCE, it grew through trade and transformed into a city-state, governed by a king and a senate. The monarchy ended with the birth of the Roman Republic in 509 BCE, when the senate became the highest authority.

Rome extended its territory throughout the Mediterranean, with its rulers waging war to maintain the city's dominance in trade. During his rule, Julius Caesar also conquered other territories. After a period of civil war, Rome became an empire in 27 BCE, and remained that way until 476 CE.

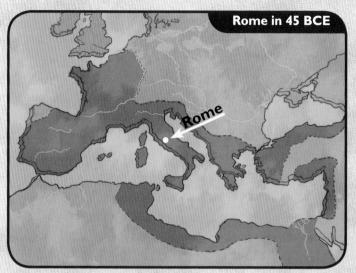

Rome in 45 BCE

Rome

The Roman territories during Julius Caesar's reign

SPQR

Many different languages were spoken in the Roman territory, but the official language during this time was Latin.

Roman monuments are often inscribed with the initials SPQR. This is an abbreviation for the phrase *Senatus populusque Romanus,* which means "the Senate and people of Rome." The Senate was made up of senators who were chosen based on their wealth and previous experience.

MEN'S ATTIRE IN ANCIENT ROME

For official occasions, men wore a toga — a long sheet wrapped around the body — but it was uncomfortable. Instead, Roman men often substituted a tunic worn with a basic woolen cloak. Their tunics often had decorative elements like stripes to highlight their wealth or class.

On their feet indoors, Roman men wore sandals with laces that laced up the calf, though they usually wore more substantial *calcei* (closed-toed shoes) outside, to protect their feet. Wealthy Romans wore brightly colored shoes, since they could afford the dyed leather.

Men in ancient Rome were required to keep their hair short and their faces freshly shaven. They each wore personalized signet rings, which they used to make impressions in sealing wax on official documents. At birth, freeborn men received a *bulla* (an amulet) that they wore on a chain around their neck until they were of age.

WOMEN'S ATTIRE IN ANCIENT ROME

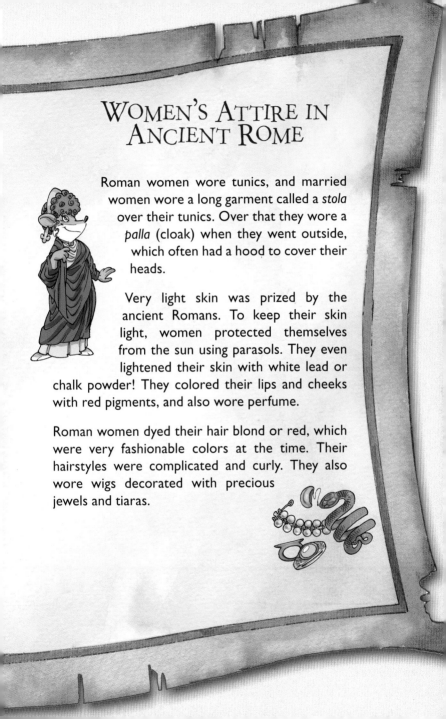

Roman women wore tunics, and married women wore a long garment called a *stola* over their tunics. Over that they wore a *palla* (cloak) when they went outside, which often had a hood to cover their heads.

Very light skin was prized by the ancient Romans. To keep their skin light, women protected themselves from the sun using parasols. They even lightened their skin with white lead or chalk powder! They colored their lips and cheeks with red pigments, and also wore perfume.

Roman women dyed their hair blond or red, which were very fashionable colors at the time. Their hairstyles were complicated and curly. They also wore wigs decorated with precious jewels and tiaras.

ANCIENT ROME . . . IN THE YEAR 45 BCE!

Our heads were spinning when we climbed out of THE RODENT RELOCATOR. Rat-munching rattlesnakes, I couldn't believe my eyes — we were really in Rome, in 45 BCE!

We quickly dressed in the CLOTHES of the ancient Romans. Then we hid the Rodent Relocator in a dark alley.

I gathered my family around. "Let's say that we are the Stiltonius family," I whispered. "We buy and sell fabric, and we're here in Rome on business."

Trap cried, "Okay,

THE ROMAN FORUM (FORUM ROMANUM)
Located in the center of the city, this main forum was an important meeting place for the Romans. Here, the Roman people would meet to buy and sell things, make important announcements, and discuss politics.

everyone, try to look **normal**! Especially you, Geronimo. After all, you always look a little . . . strange!" Then he winked and **TUGGED** my tail.

I rolled my eyes and clenched my paws. I knew he was only kidding, but Trap's jokes always get on my nerves!

But as we walked around the corner, I forgot all about being annoyed. We were in the **Roman Forum**!

The street was **PAVED** with cobblestones. Carriages and horses passed by. The smell of **SPICES** wafted out of a small shop. Two mice out front were arguing in Latin, which I knew was the official language of Rome. Thanks to my **SPECIAL** earpiece, I could understand everything they said.

"Marius, I'll pay you these silver sestertii for those olives, but only because it's you."

"Titus, because I like you, I'll cut you a deal and sell them to you for double what you're offering."

"Let's settle in the middle!"

When the deal was done, the seller mouse yelled out to Trap. "Hey, you! Stranger! If you just arrived here in **Rome**, let me offer you a Roman specialty: the mythical **GARUM**!" He pulled out a container with a thick cloud of flies around it.

> **GARUM**
> This fish sauce was a staple of ancient Roman cooking. It was made by layering fish and salt in the sun until they fermented. (Sometimes just the fish intestines were used!) It had a very, very strong taste!

Trap murmured, "**GARUM, GARUM, GARUM** . . . I like the way that word sounds. I bet it's **DELICIOUS** — I'll take some!"

I tried to stop him. "Trap, wait! We don't even know what this garum tastes like."

He snorted. "We're about to find out. We'll try some now — or rather, *you'll* try some, Gerry Berry!"

He grabbed the container, and before I could even **squeak** in protest . . .

(1) Trap poured a taste of the garum sauce in my mouth! I was so disgusted that I turned **green**. "Crusty cat litter, it tastes like rotten fish!"

(2) I ran toward a nearby fountain for a drink, but just then a horse galloped past and **crushed** my tail! "Ooooouuuuccchhh!"

(3) As I massaged my **poor** tail, a **RODENT** in one of the windows above dumped a **chamber pot** on my head. I moaned, "Why meeee?"

ON THE STREETS
OF ROME

We spent the day touring Rome. It was a
fabumouse and exciting city, but it was also
CHAOTIC! Just like in New Mouse City, we had
to be careful crossing the street, and there were
even crowded, multistory apartment
buildings called *insulae*. And it was
NOISY, too, like the cities on Mouse
Island! Even though we were far in the
past, not everything was different.

As Trap, Thea, and Benjamin walked through
the fish market, I rested my paws and waited
for them near a fountain. The sun
was already setting.

I saw a golden *lectica* — a portable couch —
being carried by four mice. It even had a roof

and curtains. A *fancy* mouse sitting on the couch looked down on everyone below. She wore golden rings on her fingers, shimmering bracelets on her wrists, and a **RUBY** crown on her head.

We want your jewels!

As I watched, a gang of bandits appeared from a dark alley and yelled, "Rich matron, give us your jewels!"

Heeeeelp!

The frightened mice dropped the couch and ran. The rich matron froze, terrified and surrounded by bandits. She squeaked, "**Heeeeelp!**"

I stepped forward. "Leave the lady alone!"

The bandits turned and

Leave the lady alone!

Scram!

Get back!

Go!

glared at me. "Get lost, rat, or we'll teach you a **lesson**!"

They narrowed in on me — but luckily, Benjamin, Thea, and Trap appeared at my side!

Benjamin threw an apple from his basket at the bandits, and they scattered in surprise.

Thea ran after them, yelling indignantly, "SCRAM, you horrible **sewer rats**! *Vade retro!** We female mice can also defend ourselves!"

Trap waved a large wooden club in the air. "Go!"

The bandits disappeared into the darkness faster than mice on a cheese hunt. **WHEW!**

The matron sobbed. "I don't

* "Get back!" in Latin.

know how to thank you — you **saved** me!"

I kissed her paw. "Madam, please don't worry. You're safe now."

She threw her paws in the air. "The goddess Juno, protector of women, must have sent you to me! Come to my *domus.** I will do my best to repay you."

We lifted the couch and followed the matron's directions to her home.

Finally, we arrived at a luxurious villa. It was a typical Roman *domus*, complete with marble decorations and covered with fancy frescoes and mosaics.

WOMEN IN ANCIENT ROME

Traditionally, Roman women were financially supported by their father, their husband, or by a close male relative. They were respected and listened to within the family, and valued mainly as wives and mothers. A married woman was called a matron.

* House

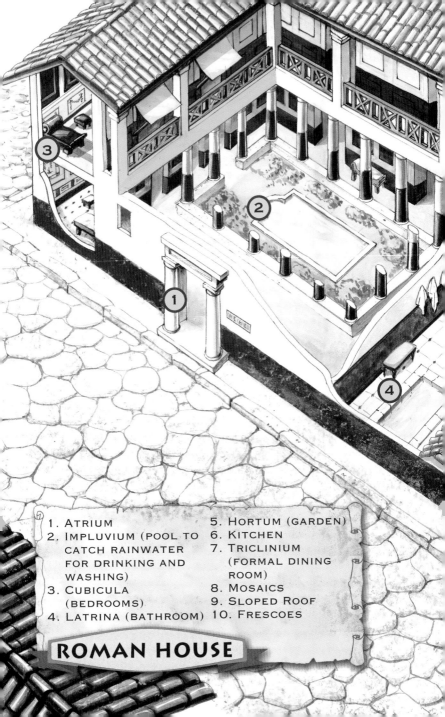

1. Atrium
2. Impluvium (pool to catch rainwater for drinking and washing)
3. Cubicula (bedrooms)
4. Latrina (bathroom)
5. Hortum (garden)
6. Kitchen
7. Triclinium (formal dining room)
8. Mosaics
9. Sloped Roof
10. Frescoes

ROMAN HOUSE

AT CAIUS MOUSILIANUS'S HOUSE

Outside the door, there was a **mosaic** with a warning: *Cave canem*!* Squeak!

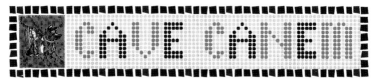

We entered the atrium (courtyard) and walked by the impluvium (a pool for gathering rainwater). All around us were *cubicula* (bedrooms). Then there was a *latrina* (bathroom), and private thermal baths. Alongside that was the *hortum* (garden), where you could walk around in the fresh air.

We passed the kitchen, and finally arrived at the *triclinium* (formal dining room).

---

* Beware of the dog.

A noble Roman ran up to us, yelling, "**Pompea!** My beloved wife!" ♥

The matron cried, "Mousilianus, my dear, these rodents saved my life!"

I introduced myself. "*Ave,** my name is *Geronimus Stiltonius*!"

Mousilianus looked at me suspiciously. "Where are you from, Stiltonius? Are you a BARBARIAN?"

I shook my snout. "Noble Mousilianus, *civis romanus sum.*** I come from Ostia, and —"

Luckily, **Pompea** interrupted. "My dear husband, let's have a banquet to CELEBRATE my escape and thank these **BRAVE** mice! *Sursum corda!****"

We all lounged on comfortable couches.

BARBARIANS AND CITIZENS

The term "barbarian" can mean someone who is uncivilized, uncultured, or a foreigner. In the Roman territory, many barbarians with lesser rights lived alongside the *cives romani* (Roman citizens). Being a Roman citizen was a privilege, and a reason to be proud.

SPQR

* Hello   ** I am a Roman citizen.   *** Lift up your hearts!

It felt so good to put my paws up! Speedy servants brought out lots of *delicious* food, including sweet, juicy fruits served on gold and silver platters. They poured us drinks in metal and terra-cotta cups.

There were so many STRANGE foods to try — and luckily, they were all whisker-licking good (though not as cheesy as I would have liked)! We ate soft-boiled eggs in pine-nut sauce, roasted wild boar, boiled ostrich, and fried veal.

Trap sighed happily, rubbing his belly. "My favorite part is how everyone eats with their paws here."

I **sighed**, looking at my messy paws. "Unfortunately, they don't seem to have invented napkins yet." (1)

Trap snickered and turned to me. "Do you mind if I just wipe my **paws** here, on your toga?"

ROMAN MEALS
The wealthier citizens of ancient Rome had two main meals: a small midday meal called the *prandium*, and a larger meal later in the afternoon called the *cena*. In the morning, they ate bread, cheese, or olives.

The poorer citizens of Rome often ate a porridge made of boiled wheat, with any vegetables, herbs, or meat they could find mixed in to enrich the flavor!

"Stop!" I yelped. That cousin of mine was always causing trouble! (2)

As Trap continued eating, I handed him a golden basin filled with water and rose petals. "Take the basin," I said. (3)

He drank the water and licked his lips. "Thanks — **THAT'S DELICIOUS!**"

"What are you doing?!" I squeaked. (4)

"What?" Trap asked innocently. "I thought you'd gotten me something to drink."

I sighed and rolled my eyes. "No, no, no — it's for washing your paws!" 5

Trap burped. "It even helped me digest!"

I shook my head in **disgust**. "Ugh — how rude!" 6

The food kept coming for hours and hours. Finally, **DESSERT** arrived: walnut-and-fig cake. Yum! I was so full, I could barely move.

Luckily, Mousilianus invited us to stay with them that night. We were all grateful. It's always nice to make new friends!

Who knew what awaited us the next day? I, for one, was too tired to worry about it. As soon as my snout hit the pillow . . . **ZZZZ**!

I'LL GIVE YOU A THERMAL BATH!

The next morning, while my family was still sleeping, Mousilianus sent for me.

"Dear Geronimus, I would like you to accompany me to my favorite *thermae,**" he said with a SMILE. "We're going to the most luxurious establishment in the city. *Carpe diem!***"

When we reached the thermal baths, I looked around and sighed happily. The thermal baths were all about **cleanliness** and hygiene, a place where most Romans went every day. I really thought I'd finally get a chance to relax!

Oh, how wrong I was!

As we entered, I admired the great marble rooms decorated with mosaics and frescoes. Some pools were **hot**, and others were **cold**. There

---

* Thermal baths   ** Seize the day!

were saunas and steam baths, gyms, and many different beauty treatments to try. To my surprise, there were even *libraries*. Cheese niblets, this was my kind of place!

Mousilianus called over a mouse who was as **BIG** as a car, as **MUSCULAR** as a bodybuilder, and as threatening as a pirate.

He told him, "Brutus, my friend Geronimus here is a very important rodent. I want you to give him *special treatment*!"

Brutus nodded. "I'll take care of it, noblest Mousilianus!"

Help!

I'll take care of it!

1. ENTRANCE
2. CHANGING ROOM
3. FRIGIDARIUM (COLD BATHS)
4. TEPIDARIUM (WARM ROOM)
5. CALIDARIUM (HOT BATHS)
6. CHANGING ROOM
7. FRIGIDARIUM

8. CALIDARIUM
9. TEPIDARIUM
10. BATHROOMS
11. SAUNA
12. POOL
13. GYM
14. CHANGING ROOM

ROMAN THERMAL BATHS

 COMMON AREAS MEN WOMEN

Brutus made me wear a ridiculously tiny towel (a little *too* tiny, if you ask me). ①

He closed me in a **hot** room (a little *too* hot, if you ask me) to purify me with steam. ②

Then he pushed me into a pool of **cold** water (a little *too* cold, if you ask me). ③

Then he scrubbed my fur with a rough instrument (a little *too* rough, if you ask me). ④

And finally, he gave me a **FORCEFUL** massage (a little *too* forceful, if you ask me). ⑤

When he was done, I hid behind a terra-cotta vase, hoping he wouldn't find me again! ⑥ I didn't leave my hiding place until Mousilianus arrived.

When we returned to Mousilianus's *domus*, Thea, Trap, and Benjamin had finally gotten up. They yawned and asked me, "Did you have fun at the thermal baths?"

I muttered, "It was an unforgettable experience!"

WE HAVE TO HELP HIM!

By that time, it was already noon. It was October, but whew — it was HOT!

My family and I decided to take a walk in the fields. We passed a farm and saw a slave slowly turning a stone mill with olives inside. His owner stood next to him and yelled, "Work, slave! Faster!"

I ran to help the poor mouse and cried, "Aren't you ashamed of treating him like that?"

Just then, the slave fainted and FELL to the ground.

"He's just a slave!" the owner scoffed. "I'm planning to sell him tomorrow, anyway. If you care about him so much, you can buy him — actually, you can buy his whole family!"

The owner stormed back inside. I kneeled next to the **poor mouse** on the ground. "Can I do something for you, friend?"

"**W-WATER . . .**" he stammered through dry lips.

I offered him a drink. After a moment, he whispered, "Thank you, kind mouse. My name is Marcus."

Marcus told us his story:

"I owned a small vineyard, but one year it didn't rain, and so we had no crops. I couldn't pay my

Woe is me!

taxes, so my family and I all ended up as **slaves**. My wife, Licia, and my seven mouselings will all be sold at the slave market tomorrow afternoon!" Tears trickled down his snout.

Benjamin squeaked, "I'm so sorry, Marcus!"

The slave wiped his **EYES** with his paw. "One of my sons is about your age, little one. Oh, *me miserum*!*"

Marcus got to his paws and began turning the milling stone again. "A slave here has no right to anything — not even friends! I'm just a poor, UNLUCKY mouse."

I couldn't believe my ears. I gathered my family around. "How terrible! We have to **help** him!" I said.

Thea whispered, "Yes, but to do that we need *pecunia*.**"

---

* Woe is me!   ** Money

DINING OUT

There were very few restaurants in ancient Rome, but many shops and taverns that served food. There were also the *thermopolia*, shops where you could buy hot food — similar to today's fast-food joints!

Benjamin nodded and added, "Lots and lots of pecunia . . ."

After saying goodbye to Marcus, we continued on our **walk** and tried to devise a plan to help him. We came across a shop and decided to get something to eat. The owner offered us bread, cheese, and sausage. Yum!

As we ate, we heard a trumpet blast. A herald announced, "Tomorrow morning in the Circus Maximus, there will be a great chariot race! Riders in horse-drawn carts will complete a dangerous, high-speed

Hear ye! Hear ye!

Pah-pa-rah!

race around the track. The winner will receive a prize of five hundred *aurei** from the highest Caesar!"

Trap cried, "I have a fabumouse idea! Tomorrow morning, SOMEONE will participate in the chariot race and win. Then, we can free Marcus. And by someone, I mean you, *Geronimo*!" He put an arm around my shoulders and grinned.

"Me?" I said with a groan. "Putrid cheese puffs, why is it always ME?"

Thea winked. "Oh, Geronimo, you should be happy. Think of the GREAT REPUTATION you'll have here if you win!"

I twisted my tail into a knot. "Instead, I'm thinking about the HORRIBLE IMPRESSION I'll make here if I lose!"

Benjamin tugged at my tunic. "Uncle, please? Win the race for me! I know you can do it!"

Why me?

* Golden coins

A SUPER-SNOOTY RODENT

The next morning, we went out to buy **armor**, a **chariot**, and two **HORSES** before the race. We didn't have much money, so we had to settle for used gear and two friendly but shabby old horses. Rancid ricotta! How was I ever going to **win** the chariot race? I'd be lucky to finish it!

Before the race, I looked at my gear. "I'm doomed!" I yelped in panic.

Trap winked. "Never fear, Cousin. To **LIFT** your spirits before the race, I'll tell you a few **JOKES** . . ."

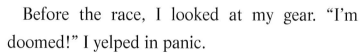

I have to admit — Trap can be hilarious!

ROMAN JOKES

CAESARS

Q: How was the Roman Empire divided?

A: With a pair of Caesars!

WORDS OF ENCOURAGEMENT

Q: What did the mouse say after he won the chariot race?

A: "That was toga-ly awesome!"

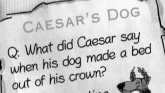

THE NOSE KNOWS

Q: What did one mouse say to the other as they walked through the Forum?

A: "Wow, smell all of those delicious a-Rome-as!"

GOOD NEWS AND BAD NEWS!

A group of mice was rowing a Roman ship. The captain said, "I have good news and bad news! The good news is that Julius Caesar has arrived. The bad news is . . . that he wants to go waterskiing!"

CAESAR'S DOG

Q: What did Caesar say when his dog made a bed out of his crown?

A: "Quit resting on my laurels!"

As we were laughing, Trap gave me some advice. "Stay in line, but during the second-to-last lap, start your comeback. A hundred meters before the **finish line**, just push through and win!"

Just then, a super-snooty rodent walked up. He was tall, muscular, and wore GOLDEN armor. His chariot was sparkling and new, with a family crest painted on it, and his horses were elegant thoroughbreds.

These are your horses?

Ha, ha, ha!

RATTILIUS
SEWERIUS

GERONIMUS
STILTONIUS

Right away, the mouse snickered and rolled his eyes at my horses. "These are your horses? Did you bring them over when they finished plowing the fields? **Ha, ha, ha!**"

The rodent laughed at my chariot, too. "And this is supposed to be your chariot? What an old piece of **junk**! Does it date back to the founding of Rome? Ha, ha, ha!"

Then he laughed at **ME**, too! "And you're supposed to be a rider? You can't be serious. Take my word for it: I, the noble Rattilius Sewerius, am going to win the **great chariot race**!"

What a bully!

I tried not to get my tail in a twist, and instead responded proudly, "May the best mouse win!"

Rattilius turned **red** and hissed, "BE CAREFUL, RAT. CAREFUL, CAREFUL, CAREFUL!"

LET THE RACE BEGIN!

Before I knew it, we all lined up in the starting gates of the **CIRCUS MAXIMUS**, near the great Roman leader Julius Caesar's stage. Caesar himself gave the signal to begin! The horses darted forward in a huge **cloud of dust**.

Ready or not, I was riding in the great chariot race!

CIRCUS MAXIMUS

This large Roman racetrack seated as many as 250,000 spectators! It was home to chariot races and other events like the Roman games. The racing chariots ran seven fast and dangerous laps counterclockwise. The finish line was right in front of the stage, where the honored guests sat.

It wasn't long before Rattilius swerved and made one chariot run off course. He pretended he was slowing down and rear-ended another **CHARIOT**. He even whipped another contestant's horse!

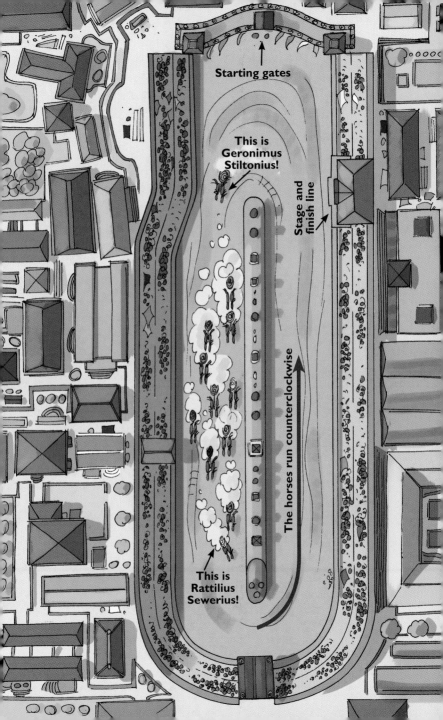

Starting gates

This is Geronimus Stiltonius!

Stage and finish line

The horses run counterclockwise

This is Rattilius Sewerius!

One at a time, he got rid of all the other contestants . . .

. . . **except me!**

Rattilius glared at me and bellowed at the **top of his lungs**, "Bring it on, rat!" Then he whipped his horses mercilessly.

I was very, very, verrrrry afraid! But just then, I heard a familiar squeak from the stands. "Come on, Uncle Geronimo!" Benjamin was cheering me on!

Instead of whipping my horses, I patted and encouraged them. "I believe in you! I know you can do it! Together, **WE WILL WIN THIS RACE**!"

The horses ran with all their might.

With just one more lap to go, we were right behind Rattilius!

Entering the last curve, he tried all of his *tricks* to fend me off, but I didn't give up.

We were getting close to the finish line. I sped up . . . and took the lead! Rattilius was **TREMBLING** with anger.

He used his chariot to shove mine up against the wall of the track. I heard a horrible **cracking** sound. He was crushing me against the wall!

The crowd gasped, "Ooooooh!"

I quickly **PULLED** at the reins and slowed down my horses, letting Rattilius pull ahead. But then I passed him on the right, picked up speed, and crossed the finish line. Applause roared in my ears. "Hooray, Geronimus Stiltonius!"

Holey cheese, I had won!

YOU ARE A BRAVE RODENT!

Happy as a mouse in a vat of melted cheese, I climbed down from my chariot, waved to the crowd, and approached the stage. Gaius Julius Caesar looked me up and down **CAREFULLY**. He murmured, "**Rotten rat's teeth!** I would never have imagined that the famous Rattilius Sewerius would be defeated by a foreigner!" He narrowed his eyes. "What is your name again?"

I gulped. Was Caesar angry?

His eyes were as cold as an **icicle**. Rancid ricotta, I was terrified!

I **stuttered**, "My name is *Giltonius Steronimus* — I mean, Geronius Stiltomerus — I mean — basically, it's Geronimus Stiltonius!"

Caesar **STARED** and **STARED** and

GAIUS JULIUS CAESAR

Caesar served as a soldier and orator before rising to political power in ancient Rome. He established a business arrangement with senators Pompey and Crassus, now referred to as the first triumvirate. Together, they effectively ruled Rome! He also extended his power with a number of conquests, taking over in places like the province of Gaul (which is now France and parts of Belgium, Germany, and Italy).

In 49 BCE, the Senate became frightened by his great power, and ordered him to relinquish his command. Instead, Caesar crossed the Rubicon River and marched on Rome, beginning a civil war that ended with the defeat of Pompey. With that, he became the most powerful man in all of Rome. He was killed on March 15, 44 BCE, thanks to a conspiracy between senators Brutus and Cassius.

ROMAN MYTHOLOGY

JUPITER (ZEUS)
King of the gods, and ruler of the Earth and the heavens

JUNO (HERA)
Jupiter's wife. Goddess of matrimony, protector of Rome, and queen of the gods

MINERVA (ATHENA)
Goddess of wisdom, the arts, science, trade, and war

MARS (ARES)
God of war and strength

ROMAN GODS

The Romans believed in many gods, who governed human actions. They imagined them as humans, with feelings like ours — love, hate, jealousy, and so on. They even dedicated marvelous temples to them! Many of the gods in Roman mythology come from Greek mythology; the names of their Greek counterparts are in parentheses above.

VENUS (Aphrodite)
Goddess of love and beauty

MERCURY (Hermes)
Messenger of the gods and
god of commerce

NEPTUNE (Poseidon)
God of the sea

DIANA (Artemis)
Goddess of fertility
and of the hunt

APOLLO (Apollo)
God of light and prophecy

VESTA (Hestia)
Goddess of the
home and hearth

STARED at me. I wanted to lower my gaze, but I resisted.

I held his magnetic gaze for what seemed like forever.

Then Caesar smiled. "You really are very **BRAVE**! I like courage in a mouse." He sniffed and asked, "And your opponent? What should we do with him? As the winner, you may **decide** what to do with his life!"

Double-twisted rat tails! It was up to **ME** if this mouse was going to live or die? That was a lot of **power** to give to a victor!

A deep silence fell over the crowd. Everyone was waiting to hear what I would say.

I didn't even have to **THINK** about my

LAUREL WREATH
The laurel wreath had no economic value, but it was a highly valued symbol of triumph. It was also considered the emblem of Apollo, the god of light.

answer. "I ask for Rattilius to be spared!" I squeaked.

Caesar nodded at me. "You are brave, and also generous!"

Caesar placed a wreath of laurel leaves on my head. Then he announced to the public, "Let us pay homage to Geronimus Stiltonius!"

Everyone in the Circus Maximus gave me a standing ovation. **"HOORAY! HOORAY!"**

I left the Circus Maximus surrounded by a giant crowd. Suddenly, someone pinched my tail, and I turned with a jump!

It was Trap, yelling, "Quickly, Cousin! If we want to save Marcus, we need to get to the slave market as **FAST** as our paws will take us. It's already three in the afternoon!"

My family and I raced to the slave market in the Forum. The slaves all were standing on a **PLATFORM**. But where was Marcus? Were we too late?

HOW MUCH DOES YOUR FREEDOM COST?

Suddenly, I spotted Marcus on a platform, a sad and resigned expression on his snout. But as soon as he spotted me, his eyes **lit up** with hope!

I snuck up to him, opened the leather bag that contained the gold coins I'd won, and whispered, "How much does your *freedom* cost?"

He took a breath. **"Twenty aurei!"**

I placed the money in his paws and asked, "And your **wife's** freedom?"

"Twenty aurei!" he responded, his eyes wide.

I put a bunch of money aside and continued, "And for your seven **children**?"

Marcus shook from ears to tail. **"SEVENTY AUREI!**

MARCUS AND HIS FAMILY

MARCUS AND HIS WIFE

THEIR SEVEN CHILDREN

THEIR CLOSE AND DISTANT RELATIVES

I can't believe I'm going to be able to buy our freedom! It seems like a dream . . ."

I smiled at Marcus, but he lowered his eyes. "Is everything all right?" I asked.

Marcus seemed embarrassed. "Um, there's also my father, Aurelius, and my mother, Gliceria, who are thirty aurei, together!"

I put another pile of money aside.

"And my wife's elderly mother, Antonia — fifteen aurei."

I sorted another pile of golden coins.

Finally, Thea exclaimed, "Marcus, if you have OTHER relatives that need freeing, just say so! We're here to help you."

Marcus cleared his throat. "Well, there is also my uncle Balbinus, my aunt Diana, and my cousin Caius! SIXTY AUREI total!"

Trap muttered, "Anyone else?"

Marcus, **RED** in the snout, **CONFESSED**, "Um, also my very distant cousin Pius. **Twenty aurei**. But that's all! "

I counted the money that was left in my bag.

I offered all of the MONEY to Marcus. "You'll need this to buy your Vineyard

> **SLAVERY**
> Roman slaves worked in the home, the fields, the factories, or the shops. Slaves could be prisoners of war, slaves bought outside Roman territory, or Roman citizens who had become slaves because of debts. The slaves were permitted to buy their own freedom if they had enough money. The possibility of freedom led most slaves to be extremely hardworking!

back. That way, you can live in peace with your family."

Marcus's eyes widened. "But there will be none left for you!" he whispered.

I smiled. "There's nothing I could buy that would be more precious than your freedom. Be happy, Marcus. And always remember us."

He hugged me, tears running down his snout.

"How could I ever forget you? Not only have you given me my freedom, but you have taught me the value of friendship!"

Trap interrupted, "This is nice and all, but *tempus fugit** — we really need to go!"

I sighed. "A very long and **DANGEROUS** journey awaits us. But we'll always be tied by friendship!"

Marcus threw his arms around me. "May **Mercury**, the god of travels, protect you!"

Omnia vincit amor!
Love conquers all!

* Time flies.

I hugged him back. *"Vale!*"*

Before leaving, we said good-bye to Mousilianus and his wife. Then we returned to the dark alley where we had hidden **THE RODENT RELOCATOR**. Luckily, no one had noticed it!

We climbed aboard and buckled in. I immediately entered our next destination into the **MICRO MOUSE**: **The Maya city of Chichén Itzá!**

The capsule began to turn and turn and turn and turn . . . and turn and turn and turn and turn

Finally, the vibrations **SLOWED**. The **MICRO MOUSE** on my wrist informed us, *"DESTINATION APPROACHING!"*

The Rodent Relocator stopped, and the Micro Mouse announced, *"DESTINATION REACHED! WE HAVE ARRIVED AT THE YUCATÁN RAIN FOREST, ON MARCH 20, 1005 CE!"*

* Farewell!

MAYA
CIVILIZATION

EXPLORATION OF THE AMERICAS

MEXICO

① San Salvador

②

Aztec

Yucatán

Guatemala

Columbus's ships

ATLANTIC OCEAN

THE YUCATÁN AND GUATEMALA: This is where the Maya lived!

PACIFIC OCEAN

SOUTH AMERICA

Inca

③

THE ARRIVAL OF THE EUROPEANS

① Christopher Columbus (In 1492, he landed on the island of San Salvador.)

② Hernán Cortés (In 1521, he conquered the Aztec people.)

③ Francisco Pizarro (In 1533, he defeated the Inca.)

THE GREAT PRE-COLUMBIAN CIVILIZATIONS

A number of civilizations developed in Central and South America before Columbus arrived in 1492. Some of the most notable include the Olmec and the Maya civilizations, some of the earliest pre-Columbian civilizations, later joined by the Toltec and Aztecs. The Inca presence in Peru began after 1100 CE.

THE MYSTERIOUS MAYA

The Maya lived mainly along the Yucatán Peninsula (now Mexico, Guatemala, and part of Belize). Their society was divided into nobles, priests, commoners, and slaves. They didn't have a clear capital city. Instead, they had many city-states, including Chichén Itzá, Tikal, Copán, Palenque, and Uxmal.

THE AZTEC WARRIORS

The capital city of the Aztec was Tenochtitlán. They conquered the territories in what is now central and southern Mexico before being defeated by Cortés in 1521. He took their ruler, Montezuma, hostage. Montezuma eventually died under uncertain circumstances.

Montezuma

THE UNLUCKY INCA

Inca civilization centered around the capital city of Cuzco (now in Peru), at one point the richest city in the New World. The Inca religion was based on sun worship, as the people worshiped the sun god, Inti. After his arrival in the Americas, Pizarro defeated the Inca and acquired a huge amount of wealth.

COLUMBUS'S ADVENTUROUS VOYAGE

CHRISTOPHER COLUMBUS

CHRISTOPHER COLUMBUS (1451–1506) received three ships (the *Niña*, the *Pinta*, and the *Santa Maria*) from the Spanish monarchy so that he could explore the Indies. Instead, on October 12, 1492, he landed on an island in the Bahamas called San Salvador. He didn't even realize that he had ended up on a new continent!

A New Continent

The continent that Columbus first landed on was soon named America, likely in honor of Amerigo Vespucci, who explored South America between 1499 and 1501.

Before long, Spanish soldiers and explorers called conquistadors were sent to the Americas. They pillaged the gold and silver of the locals (Maya, Aztec, and Inca), and enslaved their people. Even their precious works of art were destroyed at the hands of the conquistadors. As a result, these early Central and South American civilizations remain very mysterious.

MAP OF THE YUCATÁN PENINSULA

The **YUCATÁN** is a large peninsula in the Gulf of Mexico where the Maya once lived. Much of the peninsula is mountainous and covered by thick jungle and rain forest. According to legend, the name Yucatán actually came from a misunderstanding. When the Spaniards asked the locals the name of their land, the locals responded in their native tongue, saying "We don't understand you!" — and their answer sounded like the word "Yucatán." From that point on, the Spaniards called the territory Yucatán!

THE REAL TREASURE
OF THE MAYA

The door of the Rodent Relocator opened, and we all climbed out. We quickly dressed in our Maya clothing and hid the capsule. On the Micro Mouse I read, "We are in the tropical **rain forest** of the **YUCATÁN**! Here, the Maya find **fruits** to eat, **WOOD** to build their huts, **ANIMALS** to hunt, and **herbs** to make medicines. For the Maya, the forest is a source of life! They consider **NATURE** to be their greatest treasure, and they respect it greatly . . ."

I sat down and kept reading, but immediately jumped back up. Slimy Swiss cheese — I was sitting on a stinky surprise left behind by a toucan (if you know what I mean)!

Grrrrrrrrrrr!

TROPICAL RAIN FOREST
1. Chicozapote plant
   (sapodilla)
2. Toucan
3. Quetzal
4. Boa constrictor
5. Geronimo Stilton
6. Lycaste orchid
7. Tapir
8. Jaguar
9. Stanhopea orchid
10. Black-handed spider
monkey
11. Liana

MAYA FASHION

Maya men wore loincloths (a strip of fabric wrapped around the waist). They sometimes wore a cloak over their shoulders that also served as a blanket during the night. The women often wore embroidered fabric shirts with a hole for the head and two armholes, and long skirts. Both men and women wore their hair long, except the men may have cut the sides short.

The Maya loved tattoos, and they carved into their skin using sharpened bones, penetrating the skin with colored paints.

WARRIOR

NOBLEMAN

PEASANT

CHILD

STRANGE CUSTOMS

The Maya men and women pierced their earlobes. They would enlarge the holes a bit at a time, until they could eventually insert pendants (called flares or spools) in them that could be as big as eggs! They often pierced their noses and tongues, too!

An elongated head was considered beautiful by the Maya, as was strabismus (being cross-eyed or having a lazy eye).

Maya warriors painted their bodies red and black. Blue, on the other hand, was the paint color used specifically for sacred ceremonies.

NOBLEWOMAN

PEASANT

CHILD

Armadillo

Banana

Senecio plant

Wood

I squeaked, "Putrid cheese puffs!" Because of the toucan's little surprise, my tunic was all dirty — and I didn't have a change of clothes! Rats! I had no choice. I had to continue on, leaving a stinky toucan scent everywhere I went!

I kept reading from the Micro Mouse. "The Maya don't have money. They use things like JADE, SALT, and cacao seeds as currency for trading. Cacao beans are considered extremely valuable. The Maya get chocolate from these beans, which they drink in liquid form and consider to be the FOOD OF THE GODS! With enough cacao beans, you can even buy a slave."

Thea shook her head. "There's slavery here, too? How terrible!"

The four of us set out through the forest, but after walking for a **LONG** time, the Maya city of Chichén Itzá was nowhere to be seen. My poor paws were on fire!

Thea suggested, "Someone should **climb** a tree, so we can orient ourselves. I'll stay down here and keep watch."

Jade

Cacao

Sisal

Chicozapote
(chewing gum)

FROM AMERICA

After the exploration of the Americas, many new and unknown things arrived in Europe — cacao (chocolate), coffee, sweet potatoes, corn, black beans, squash, tomatoes, papaya, avocado, and even chewing gum, which the Maya made from the gummy resin of the chicozapote plant!

Who will climb the tree?

Umm ... Umm ... Er ...

Trap agreed. "Yeah, someone definitely needs to **climb up** this tree. But I can't — I have to make us some breakfast!"

Benjamin piped up. "I'll climb it!"

Thea and Trap shook their heads. "You're too **small**. We need someone else, like . . ."

All three of them turned to look at me.

I became as **white** as a slab of mozzarella. "M-m-me?" I stammered. "But I can't climb it — I'm afraid of **HEIGHTS**!"

Thea pushed me toward the **TOWERING** tree. "Just don't look down, Geronimo. You'll be fine! *Don't look down!*"

I tried to sneak away . . .

. . . but Trap grabbed me by the tail. "What are you doing, Gerrykins? Running away?"

Benjamin insisted, "Uncle, I can climb the tree instead!"

I patted his ears. "Thanks, sweet Benjamin," I said, looking up at the tree. "But I'll do it. After all, the secret of courage is facing your fears!"

I took a deep breath and tried to think courageous thoughts.

Then I began to climb.

When I was about halfway up, I looked down . . . and my head started to spin! Moldy mozzarella, hadn't Thea told me not to look down?

I tried to stay calm, repeating, "I CAN DO THIS! I CAN DO THIS! I CAN DO THIS!"

Finally, I arrived at the top — and I couldn't believe my eyes!

A DATE . . .
WITH A JAGUAR!

From the top of the tree, I could see the Maya **pyramid**!

When I climbed down, I knew exactly which way we needed to walk. Thea and Benjamin cheered. "Good job, Geronimo!"

Trap snorted. "Yeah, but you were so scared that your tail was trembling!"

Thea gave me a hug. "Someone who is truly courageous knows how to overcome his fears. Geronimo, you were **SCARED** — but you climbed anyway!"

Cheese and crackers, I was proud of myself!

Before heading out, we decided it was time for breakfast. Trap lit a fire — but just then we heard a frightened cry coming from the

darkest part of the forest!

Then a roar echoed in the trees. **Grrrrrrr!**

Holey cheese, what was that?

I grabbed a branch and dipped it in the fire, so it would glow like a torch. Then, silently, I walked farther into the forest — until I saw two small mouselets up in a tree!

Below them was a dangerous *JAGUAR*, ready to tear them to bits! The Maya considered jaguars to be kings of the forest, and now I could see why. Rat-munching rattlesnakes, it was fierce and terrifying!

The jaguar roared, grinding its **POINTY** teeth. It grabbed the trunk of the tree with huge, sharp claws . . . and started to climb!

The mouselets squeaked in **fear**. The older one hugged his sister tight to protect her.

I had to get my tail in gear!

I ran toward the jaguar, waving my flaming **stick** and yelling at the top of my lungs.

Thea appeared behind me with a THORNY

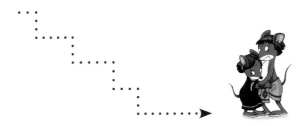

branch, and Trap ran up with a **HUGE**, sharp stone. Nearby, Benjamin banged two rocks together to scare the beast.

GRRRRRRRRRRRR!

Just like that, the jaguar forgot about the mouselings and **turned** to face us. He gnashed his teeth and opened his mouth so wide that we could see his **tonsils**. Gulp! Then, with a quick swipe, he **clawed my tail**!

I'm too fond of my tail!

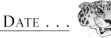

Get out of here!

Hooray!

I yelped, "No way, jaguar! I'm too fond of my tail!" I waved the FLAMING stick under his nose and singed his whiskers! Shocked by the fire, the jaguar left in a flash, his whiskers still smoking. I couldn't help cheering.

I waited until the jaguar had completely disappeared, and then I turned to the two mouselets climbing out

Thanks for saving us!

Don't be scared!

of the tree. "Hi — are you all right? My name is, um, Geronimac Stiltonax."

The ratlet smiled gratefully. "My name is **Atl**, and this is my sister, **XOCO**. We can't thank you enough for saving us. But you hurt your tail! Come to our house — our mother, Ankarat, knows how to cure injuries with herbs, and my father, Balamous, will be so happy to meet the mice who saved us!"

We agreed, and followed the mouselings until we reached the edge of the forest and could see . . .

"**Chichén Itzá!**" I cried in excitement.

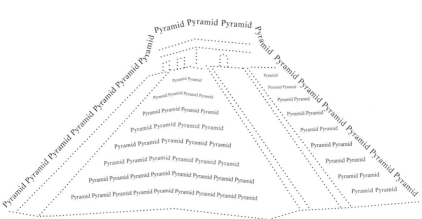

WELCOME TO CHICHÉN ITZÁ!

We had finally arrived in **Chichén Itzá**, the great Maya city!

The last rays of sun lit up the golden sky overhead. A majestic pyramid stood before us, looking like solid gold in the sunlight. It was a fabumouse sight!

The city was surrounded by a protective **STONE** wall. All around it, we could see many thatched huts.

Atl and Xoco led us to one of these wooden huts and yelled, "Dad! Mom!"

Two mice ran out to greet us.

Atl explained, "A *JAGUAR* chased us, but this stranger **saved our lives**!"

Balamous fell to his knees before me. "Thank

you for saving my children, brave rodent! What can I do for you? I'll give you anything you ask!"

I smiled. "I'm **happy** to have helped your mouselings. You don't owe me anything."

Balamous stood up, a tear in his eye. He clasped my paw and said, "Welcome to Chichén Itzá, noble stranger!"

OUR HOME
IS YOUR HOME!

Maya home

Balamous looked down at his PAWS sheepishly. "I'm afraid that we are poor peasants, and our house is nothing much. But we offer you everything we have with all our heart! *Our home is your home!*"

The hut was small, and inside, the clay ground was covered with leaf mats. In one corner, there was a basket of **dried beans**, a pile of RIPE PAPAYA, and a bowl of honey. Seeing the honey, I remembered that the Maya raised **Maya bees**, a special species of bee that can't sting!

Maya bee

Balamous insisted, "Please stay! We will have a banquet in your honor!"

Peasants from the NEIGHBORING huts all came to the banquet. Each one brought something different to eat: CORN bread, **BLACK BEAN** bread, **baked** sweet potatoes, stuffed **PUMPKIN**, spicy iguana, **ARMADILLO** stew, **Hare** roast, and a BANANA dessert.

Trap cried, "Okay, everyone, try to look normal! Especially you, Geronimo. After all, you always look a little . . . strange!" Then he winked and tugged my tail.

I rolled my eyes and clenched my paws. I knew he was only kidding, but Trap's jokes always get on my nerves!

During dinner, Balamous told us a legend about jaguars.

It was a fascinating story! As I listened, I **distractedly** grabbed a bowl with some red liquid inside.

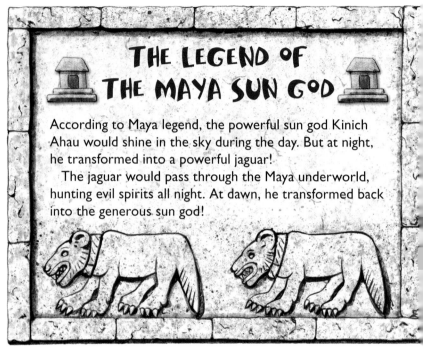

THE LEGEND OF THE MAYA SUN GOD

According to Maya legend, the powerful sun god Kinich Ahau would shine in the sky during the day. But at night, he transformed into a powerful jaguar!

The jaguar would pass through the Maya underworld, hunting evil spirits all night. At dawn, he transformed back into the generous sun god!

I thought it was tomato sauce, so I swallowed it in one gulp.

My eyes *BURST* open!

My tongue caught fire!

SMOKE came out of my ears!

Ankarat **squeaked**, "Careful! Watch out for the hot pepper!"

Double-twisted rat tails — too late!

When my mouth finally stopped **burning** and the last guest left the banquet, we all lay down on leaf mats. We wrapped ourselves in **brightly colored** blankets and fell asleep, tired but happy.

Yum!

Aaaack!

Glub!

Huh?

WATCH OUT FOR THE HOT PEPPER!

DAWN IN THE MAYA VILLAGE

It was four in the morning when I woke up. Ankarat was making corn tortillas.

Balamous announced, "Today is the **FESTIVAL OF SPRING**, an extremely special day! Chichén Itzá is a **sacred city**, and the festival of spring is cause for great celebration. As the sun moves across the sky today, it will look like a giant snake of light is gliding down the Pyramid of Kukulcán's main steps."

Light the fire ...

make the dough ...

lay it on a fiery stone!

On our way into the city, I spotted many artisanal shops. Many of the Maya utensils I spotted — razors, mirrors, and knives — were made of **OBSIDIAN**, a hard volcanic glass!

CORN
The Maya dried, husked, and boiled their corn. Then they ground it in a stone mortar to create a dough, which they used to make corn tortillas. These were a staple of Maya meals!

The women weaved fabrics and gathered sisal from the agave plant to make rope and textiles. They also created fabumouse headdresses using colorful feathers from birds, and made beautiful decorative vases.

Maya loom

POP

WO'

ZIP

ZOTZ'

K'ANK'IN

MUWAN'

PAX

THE MAYA CALENDAR

These symbols represent the nineteen sections of the Maya Haab calendar: eighteen months of twenty days each, plus an extra period of five days (called "Wayeb"). These were used as a time to reflect and prepare for the new calendar cycle. This version of the Maya calendar is similar to our own 365-day calendar, though it is broken up differently. It's made up of a complex system of interlocking wheels!

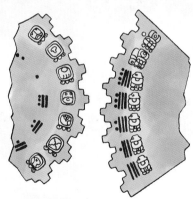

KA'YAAB

KUM'KU

WAYEB'

TZEK

XUL

YAXK'IN

MOL

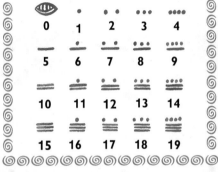

CH'EN

YAX

The Maya numbers were represented by lines and dots, and the zero was like a shell. These numbers indicated the days of the month. For example, 0 Pop, 1 Pop, 2 Pop (with the lines and dots above standing in for the corresponding numbers), and so on.

MAK

KEH

ZAK

THE SWEAT BATH

Balamous led us to a stone building that reminded me of a pizza oven. (Mmmm, pizza . . .)

"Before visiting the **sacred city**, it is Maya tradition to have a sweat bath, to purify your body and spirit." He handed five cacao seeds to a kind-looking mouse of the *priestly class* who introduced himself.

"I am Puuc. I run the sweat bath!"

We all undressed and wrapped our fur in white towels. Then we ducked through the little door

and entered the *hot* room.

Puuc explained, "The door is short because, to purify yourself, you must first learn how to be *humble*!"

Puuc poured some *copal* (which smelled like incense) on the fiery stones, and scented steam rose into the air. He closed the door, and we found ourselves in total **DARKNESS**!

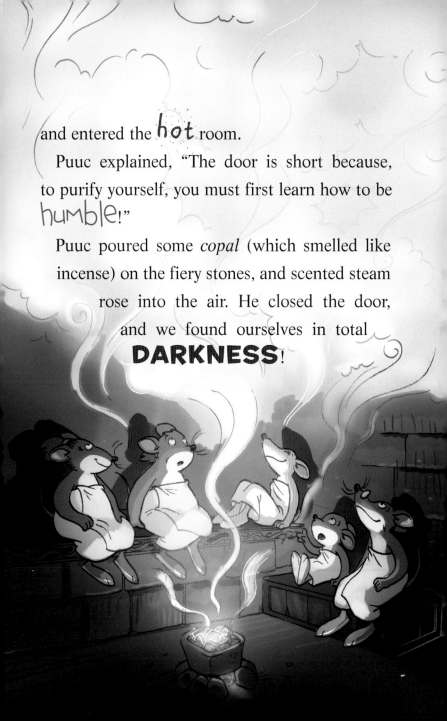

Puuc explained, "The steam will deep clean your fur. Sweating helps eliminate **toxins**, which are the waste your body produces."

The steam bath sounded a lot like the saunas we had in New Mouse City!

Puuc whispered, "Tell me if you see something in the **steam**. Based on what you see, I can tell you what it says about you!"

Once our eyes adjusted to the darkness, Thea saw an *EAGLE* with spread wings, and Puuc said, "That is a symbol of power. It means that you are a free spirit!"

Benjamin saw a **HEART**, and Puuc smiled. "You are a sensitive mouselet!"

Trap saw a slice of **melon**, which made Puuc laugh. "You only think of material objects!"

I, on the other paw, saw a CLOUD.

Puuc's face lit up. "A cloud? Really? **That's a good sign!** Maybe it will rain!"

After a little while, we said good-bye to Puuc, left the sweat bath, and got dressed again.

"Oh, I'm so clean!" I cheered. "I really like being clea —"

Just then, a **stinky** toucan **surprise** fell right on my head! 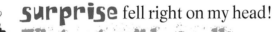  What a terrible smell!

"Putrid cheese puffs!" I squeaked.

I wanted to get cleaned up — after all, I'm a very tidy mouse! But there was no time to go back to the sweat bath. We had to continue on, stink and all.

INSIDE THE
SACRED CITY

Visiting the city was absolutely fabumouse!

I never imagined that some of the Maya monuments were originally painted in such vibrant colors. They were bright and beautiful!

We came across a large square, where there was a market.

Balamous gestured up ahead and said, "There's the Pyramid of Kukulcán! And over there is the Platform of Venus, where SACRED DANCES are performed."

Balamous led us to a huge stadium. From

> ## MAYA BLUE
> The Maya used a bright, durable blue paint in much of their art, architecture, and books. This has come to be called "Maya blue," due to its unique hue and common use on Maya ruins and artifacts. After studying it for many years, scientists only recently figured out how this color was made!

MAP of CHICHÉN ITZÁ

The name Chichén Itzá means "at the mouth of the Itzá well." The city was an important center of civilization and trade between 900 and 1200 CE. At its height, it was a significant Maya city, and many people lived in the surrounding areas.

1. The Thousand Columns
2. Temple of the Warriors
3. Pyramid of Kukulcán
4. Platform of Venus
5. Great Ball Court
6. Temple of the Jaguars
7. Observatory
8. Akabtzib temple
9. Sweat bath
10. Sacred Well

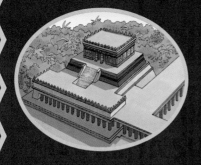

THE THOUSAND COLUMNS

TEMPLE OF THE JAGUARS

PYRAMID OF KUKULKÁN

OBSERVATORY

PLATFORM OF VENUS

AKABTZIB TEMPLE

there, we could SEE many different parts of the city.

"Now we are at the Great Ball Court," he explained. "And there is the Temple of the Jaguars, where spectators watch the GAMES. Over there, in the Observatory, mice study the secrets of the sky; and there is the Akabtzib temple, also known as the House of the **Dark Writing**!"

Balamous *pointed* out a long colonnade. "That is the Thousand Columns. Next to it is the Temple of the Warriors."

MAYA BOOKS

Maya books were written with hieroglyphics (sacred script), and were also illustrated. To create paper, the Maya softened tree bark and made it into long sheets, folded like an accordion. These are called codices.

Only three Maya books were saved from destruction when the conquistadors took over in the sixteenth century. It was a devastating loss!

The Chichén Itzá Market

POK-TA-POK!

We took some time to look around the **Great Ball Court**. It was surrounded by tall rock walls, and the court itself was 545 feet long and 223 feet wide. Holey cheese, it was **HUGE** — even bigger than a football field!

Balamous explained, "I brought you all here to attend a **sacred ball game** called *pok-ta-pok*! We take it very seriously. It's sometimes played as part of a religious ceremony, and other times it's the final combat for prisoners of war."

The game seemed a little like basketball, but harder — the rubber ball had to be hit through a **really, really small** stone ring!

HOW DID THE MAYA PLAY POK-TA-POK?

The game was played with two teams. Every player wore padding and tried to hit a heavy, hard rubber ball through a stone ring on the wall. But it was extremely difficult! The stone ring was just big enough for the ball to fit through, and was very high up. Plus, the players couldn't use their hands once the ball was in play — they could only touch it with their heads, shoulders, legs, hips, and chest! The game seems nearly impossible, and matches were said to last hours . . . or days!

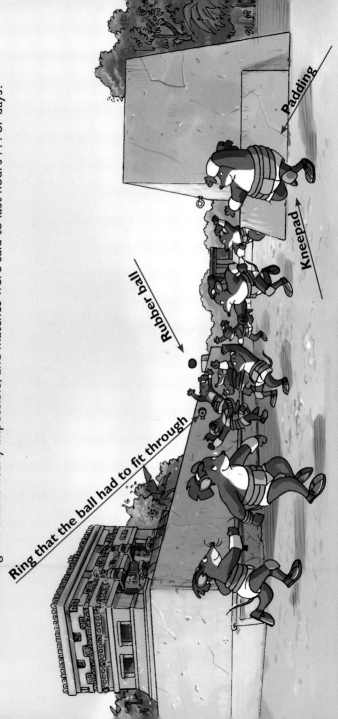

Ring that the ball had to fit through

Rubber ball

Padding

Kneepad

BUT I DON'T KNOW HOW TO DANCE!

We headed back to the market, where a group of priests were getting ready for a **SACRED DANCE**.

"Come dance with us!" one of the priests said to me.

My snout went **PALE** and my WHISKERS drooped. I have always been a **TERRIBLE** dancer! I have no sense of **rhythm** at all. When Thea forces me to waltz with her, I always accidentally stomp on her paws!

But I had no choice.

SACRED DANCES
Maya dances were a form of religious expression. Dancers waved fans and wore rattles made of branches. The sacred dances were meant to summon important gods, like the maize god and the rain spirit. They often lasted for hours — and making sure that everyone moved in unison was extremely important!

The priest pulled me up onto the stone stage where the other mice were dancing. It was part of the **Platform of Venus**!

Off to the side some of the priests were preparing for the dance by dying their fur blue and tying rattles to their knees. I went over to take a closer look.

Platform of Venus

Pyramid of Kukulcán

"What are you waiting for, Geronimo?" Trap said. "Dance!"

He gave me a **SHOVE**. I slipped on the stage and **TOPPLED** into the priest who was holding the blue dye.

Holey cheese! I was blue from head to toe!

I watched the musicians as they got ready to play. They had a variety of trumpets, bone flutes, maracas, and drums made from turtle shells.

One of the musicians lifted a **conch shell** and blew into one end.

TOOOO-TOOOO-TOOOO-BOOO-ROOOO!

That was the signal to begin the dance!

But just then, the *WIND* turned in our direction — and it brought a cloud of gnats with it!

The gnats were attracted to my horrible **stench** (thanks for nothing, toucan!) — and they began to bite me! They nibbled my ears, my snout, and even flew into my nostrils, ears, and mouth!

I'm one huge bite!

"I'm basically just one huge **BITE**!" I cried, swatting and squeaking.

I began to **JUMP** frantically back and forth, right and left, and up and down on the stage.

As I was jumping, I slipped on another stinky toucan surprise! **What a terrible smell!**

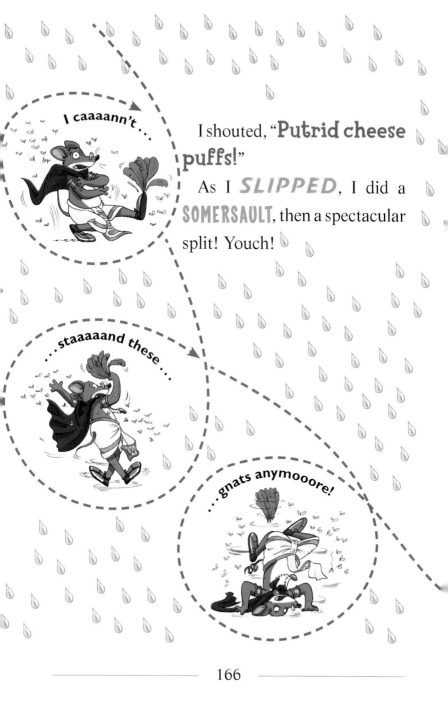

I caaaann't...

I shouted, "**Putrid cheese puffs!**"

As I *SLIPPED*, I did a **SOMERSAULT**, then a spectacular split! Youch!

...staaaaand these....

...gnats anymooore!

The mice in the crowd cried, "Wow! That Geronimac Stiltonax is a fabumouse dancer!"

As I climbed to my paws, I heard a strange noise — **thunder**!

A drop of something fell on my snout . . . another on my ear . . . and another on my whiskers.

It was **RAIN**!

Toucan surprise!

HAPPINESS IS A DROP OF RAIN!

The Maya cheered. "Foreigner, the **gods** liked your incredible dance. They made it rain!"

Moldy mozzarella, were they serious? I was pretty sure it just rained because the **CLOUDS**

Hooray for rain!

had arrived! But then I saw how happy the Maya were, so I said politely, "If that's what you think, I'm happy I could help!"

One of the priests lifted his arms and cried solemnly, "Thank you for this rain!"

The rest of the Maya ran off, singing in unison, "Thank you!"

Clearly rain was very important to them. It must have had to do with food that they grew.

I lifted my head and felt the fresh raindrops hit my snout.

I thought about how you could find HAPPINESS in everything — in BREAD when you're hungry, in a **BLANKET** when you're cold, in a **smile** when you're alone, and in a drop of **rain** when it's been dry!

The priest *kneeled* down next to me. "Foreigner, we bestow you with a GREAT honor — climbing the pyramid, where you will meet **Kukulcán**, our leader!"

Balamous sighed wistfully. "Oh, Geronimac, climbing the **pyramid** is an amazing honor! I've always wanted to climb it, so I could tell my GRANDCHILDREN all about it, and they could tell their GRANDCHILDREN, who would tell their GRANDCHILDREN, for generations and generations."

I patted Balamous on the shoulder. "Would you like to climb it with me?"

He stammered, beside himself with excitement, "G-great husks of corn! Really? That would make me the happiest mouse in the world!"

So as the **sun set** and the sky turned red, we began to climb the great pyramid . . .

grandchildren
grandchildren
grandchildren
grandchildren
grandchildren
grandchildren
grandchildren
grandchildren
grandchildren

grandchildren
grandchildren
grandchildren

So many stairs!

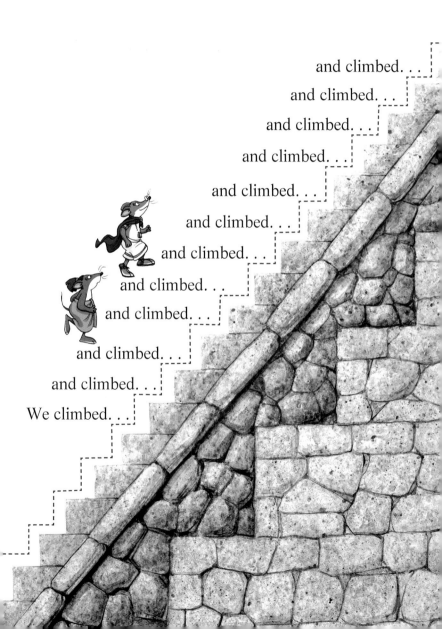

and climbed. . .

and climbed. . .

and climbed. . .

and climbed. . .

and climbed. . .

and climbed. . .

and climbed. . .

and climbed. . .

and climbed. . .

and climbed. . .

and climbed. . .

We climbed. . .

At the top of the **pyramid**, I stood before the Maya leader. The Maya considered him to be the living embodiment of Kukulcán, the feathered serpent god! He wore an elaborate yellow-and-black garment, **golden sandals**, and a very tall headdress made of GREEN FEATHERS.

He turned to me. "What would you like, foreigner, as payment for having danced your strange dance that made it rain?"

I thought for a moment before responding, but there was only one thing I really wanted. "Um, I'd like to examine the **books** of your people!"

The leader lowered his head as a sign of consent, and pointed to the Akabtzib temple.

AKABTZIB, THE HOUSE OF THE DARK WRITING!

I bowed, and we climbed down the pyramid.

We went down . . .

and down . . .

and down . . .

and down . . .

and down . . .

and down . . .

and down . . .

and down . . .

and down . . .

and down . . .

When we finally reached the ground, Balamous and the priest led me, Thea, Trap, and Benjamin to the Akabtzib temple.

The priest explained, *"Akabtzib* means 'Dark writing.' All of the knowledge of our people is recorded in our sacred books!"

I sighed with happiness. Cheese and crackers, this was a dream come true!

We entered the **TEMPLE**, and the priest pointed to the thousands of paper books all around us.

I began to flip through the long-lost books

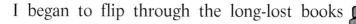

excitedly. There was so much to learn!

I was planning to photograph some of the books with the Micro Mouse — but just then, the ground began to shake!

It was an earthquake!

Trap hollered, "There's no time to study these dusty papers, Cousin — we need to leave immediately! If the Rodent Relocator is damaged by the earthquake, we'll be STUCK here forever!"

THE RODENT RELOCATOR

I squeaked in protest. "What do you mean, dusty papers? These books are full of long-lost secrets!"

Thea yelped, "Hurry!"

Benjamin pulled me by the tail. "Please, Uncle, let's go! I'm SCARED!"

I really wanted to find answers to some of the amazing Maya mysteries, but my family's

MYSTERIES OF THE MAYA

THEY ABANDONED THEIR CITIES — WHY?

Maya culture was at its peak, with strong armies and large populations located in beautiful cities. But within a hundred years or so, many of the major Maya cities were abandoned. There was no epidemic, no military invasion, and no natural disaster that we know of that would force them to leave — so why?

CALENDARS, BUT NO WHEELS — WHY?

The Maya had an amazingly accurate calendar, complex writing system, and great understanding of mathematics, but we haven't found concrete evidence that they had the wheel or the plow — why?

These mysteries are unresolved, partially because only a very small percentage of the original Maya monuments have been found. The rest are still hidden in the tropical rain forest! Much about the Maya remains a mystery, but that is what makes them so fascinating . . .

safety was much more IMPORTANT.

I squeezed Balamous's paw and wished him well. "Stay safe! We need to leave immediately, but I hope we'll be back one day. Thank you for being such a wonderful friend to us!"

The earth continued to shake under our paws, while the rain washed the blue dye from my fur.

THE MYSTERY OF THE SACRED WELL!

The sun had set, and it was nighttime.

On our way out of Chichén Itzá, we ran past a really deep well — the Sacred Well! I peeked into it just for a moment. The moon shone silver on the water at the bottom.

I got chills.

Trap LOOKED back over his shoulder and yelled, "Hurry, GERMEISTER! If you're fond of your fur, there's no time to lose!"

We left Chichén Itzá behind and sprinted

FRESHWATER WELLS

Chichén Itzá was built near natural freshwater wells called the *tzonot*, which were later called *cenotes* by the Spanish. They were an important and permanent source of surface water, and spiritually significant to the Maya. They considered the wells to be portals between the Earth and the underworld!

The Sacred Well!

back into the dense TROPICAL FOREST. The ground shook harder and harder beneath our paws!

Finally, we arrived where we'd hidden the Rodent Relocator. Luckily, the earthquake hadn't damaged it. Whew! We climbed in, buckled our seat belts, and began to spin and spin and spin . . .

The **Micro Mouse** on my wrist informed me, *"DESTINATION APPROACHING!"*

The Rodent Relocator stopped, and the Micro Mouse announced, *"DESTINATION REACHED! WE ARE IN VERSAILLES DURING THE REIGN OF THE SUN KING, SEPTEMBER 4, 1682 CE!"*

the Reign of the Sun King

THE LIFE OF THE SUN KING, LOUIS XIV

LOUIS XIV'S CHILDHOOD

Louis XIV was born on September 5, 1638 to King Louis XIII of France and his wife, Anne of Austria. He inherited the crown at four years old, officially becoming the leader of more than 19 million French subjects, but his mother and her chief minister ruled on his behalf until he was twenty-three.

As a child, Louis XIV played with toy soldiers. He would eventually go on to command some of those same armies in real life. It's said that he even had a tiny toy cannon pulled by a flea! He also played with his brother, Philippe, who was two years younger than him. Even at a very young age, the boys witnessed some serious political battles, which led to Louis XIV's lifelong fear of rebellion.

LOUIS XIV'S PERSONALITY

Louis XIV was extremely hardworking, and surrounded himself with great intellectuals and artists. He was also very cautious. He responded to many requests by saying, "*Je verrai!*" ("I will see!")

Louis XIV followed a strict, predictable routine day after day. He married Marie-Thérèse, daughter of King Philip IV of Spain, in 1660. They had five children together. Two of his main hobbies were hunting and dancing. He loved ballet!

POLITICS AND THE ECONOMY

When Louis XIV took the throne, he decided not to have a chief minister. He began to govern as an absolute monarch, and believed that he was given the power to rule directly from God.

Louis XIV is remembered as having said, "*L'État c'est moi*" ("I am the State"). He called himself the "Sun King," because he believed that the realm should revolve around him the way the planets revolve around the sun.

He engaged in various wars against the surrounding states to extend France's power and influence, but wasn't always successful. Long conflicts and excessive spending sent France into debt! After Louis XIV's death in 1715, France entered a period of decline that ultimately led to the French Revolution.

In Versailles . . .
in 1682 CE!

When we got out of THE RODENT RELOCATOR, my head was spinning like a top. I could barely see the end of my snout!

But as my vision cleared, it become obvious that we really were in *Versailles* in 1682! It was dawn on September 4.

We changed into the clothing the professor had packed for us — wigs, tights, and lace shirts. Cheesy cream puffs, we looked silly! Then we hid the Rodent Relocator behind a *rosebush* and began to explore.

But before long, we all started itching . . . and itching . . . and itching! We looked closely, and we could see tons of little *insects* happily jumping on our clothes and wigs. **Fleas!** Yuck!

Trap yelped, "Why did the professor give us clothes that were full of fleas?" Then he chuckled. "Where did he get them from, a **flea market**?"

> ### HYGIENE IN THE 1600s
> During this time, wigs and clothes were full of fleas! Instead of bathing with water, people often covered up the smell with expensive perfumes. No one brushed their teeth, which meant that many people had rotten teeth — and terrible breath! There were also no bathrooms; instead, they used chamber pots called *vases de nuit.*

A new message popped up on the **MICRO MOUSE**.

"Moldy mozzarella!" I cried. "This says that in France in the seventeenth century, mice often didn't **bathe**. And having fleas was common!"

I scratched my fur and tried to distract myself by thinking about how we should introduce ourselves to the other mice here. "We'll say that we are the Stiltoneaux family, visiting *Versailles* on vacation," I suggested.

Geronimo

Geronimo wears an elegant green outfit, including a close-fitting jacket with big gold buttons, and a curly wig. His clothing has lots of detailed embroidery.

Trap

Trap wears a refined blue jacket with gold details, dyed silk stockings, and a long, curly blond wig — complete with fleas!

Benjamin

Benjamin wears a red coat with buckles and golden embroidery, and soft shoes with bows on the front. Children during this time period often dressed like miniature adults. Their clothing made it hard to run and play.

Thea

Thea wears a brocade red dress with a corset and a tapered waist. The dress has expensive lace sleeves that go to her elbows. Thea also has a fancy hairdo and a fake beauty mark painted on her cheek.

Trap cried, "Okay, everyone, try to look normal! Especially you, Geronimo. After all, you always look a little . . . strange!" Then he winked and tugged my tail.

I rolled my eyes and clenched my paws. I knew he was only kidding, but Trap's jokes always get on my nerves!

With that, we passed through a golden gate . . .

TOGETHER, WE WALKED DOWN A LONG ROAD PAVED WITH GRAY STONES.

Finally, we arrived at the palace. It was enormouse!

A guard put up a paw to stop us. "Who are you?"

I announced, "I am *Gerôme Stiltoneaux*, and this is my family. We are here to pay homage to the Sun King!"

I took in the view. Surrounding the royal palace was an enormouse garden. Mist from the garden fountains sprayed our snouts. What a sight!

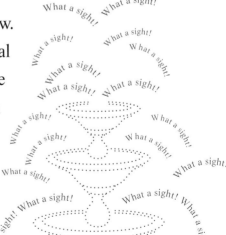

Welcome to Versailles!

VERSAILLES

Louis XIV moved his court and government to Versailles (a former royal hunting lodge about ten miles southwest of Paris) in 1682. The magnificent palace was designed by the architects Louis Le Vau, Charles Le Brun, Jules Hardouin-Mansart, and André Le Nôtre.

DID YOU KNOW?

- Louis XIV actually moved the court to Versailles so that the courtiers would be close. That way, he could keep an eye on them — and stop them from conspiring against him!
- Every day, there were between 3,000 and 10,000 people at the court.
- The king and queen had virtually no private life — their every move was watched and scrutinized by the courtiers!
- The entire Versailles estate is approximately 2,000 acres, and has 50 fountains, an orangerie with more than 1,000 trees, and a Grand Canal that's more than a mile long! The palace itself has 700 rooms, more than 2,000 windows, 1,250 chimneys, and 67 staircases. It is capable of holding up to 20,000 people!

MAP OF VERSAILLES

1. Entrance to the courtyard
2. Royal Palace
3. Water Terrace
4. Latona Fountain
5. Royal Walk
6. Fountain of Apollo
7. Grand Canal
8. Grand Trianon
9. King's Garden
10. Colonnade
11. Girandole Grove
12. Queen's Grove
13. Orangerie (orange grove)
14. Noon Terrace
15. Grove of Domes
16. Obelisk Grove
17. Dauphin's Grove
18. Star Grove
19. Water Theatre Grove
20. North Terrace
21. Pyramid Fountain
22. Water Walk
23. Three Fountains
24. Dragon Fountain
25. Neptune Fountain

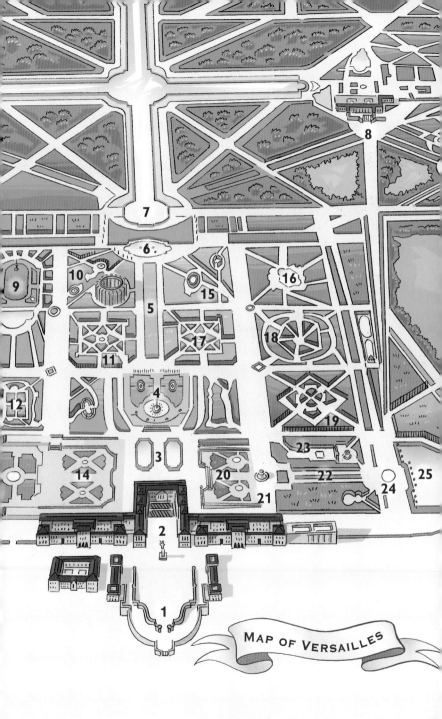

MAP OF VERSAILLES

Hall of Mirrors

1

2

3

4

9

13

10

11

12

14

Coronation Room

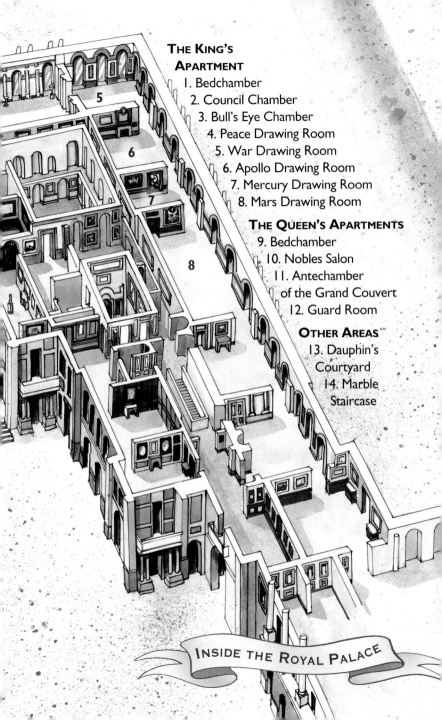

THE KING'S APARTMENT
1. Bedchamber
2. Council Chamber
3. Bull's Eye Chamber
4. Peace Drawing Room
5. War Drawing Room
6. Apollo Drawing Room
7. Mercury Drawing Room
8. Mars Drawing Room

THE QUEEN'S APARTMENTS
9. Bedchamber
10. Nobles Salon
11. Antechamber of the Grand Couvert
12. Guard Room

OTHER AREAS
13. Dauphin's Courtyard
14. Marble Staircase

INSIDE THE ROYAL PALACE

A CHAMBER POT FOR THE SUN KING!

Once the guard let us pass, we joined the crowd of courtiers filling the courtyard. Like us, they were waiting for the king to **wake up** so they could pay their respects!

It was eight o'clock when a page finally announced, "The king has opened his **EYES**!"

The crowd roared. "*Vive le roi!**"

With that, everyone **CLIMBED** the marble stairway leading to the second floor and the king's apartments.

THE SUN KING'S DAY
8:00 a.m. The king wakes up, dresses, and eats breakfast.
9:00 a.m.–12:00 p.m. He attends church, holds hearings with his subjects, and meets with his advisors.
1:00 p.m. Lunch
2:00 p.m. He relaxes, goes for a walk, hunts, or plays with his dogs.
6:00 p.m. He signs letters and studies important documents.
10:00 p.m. He dines with his family, viewed by crowds of courtiers.
11:30 p.m. The king goes to bed after a public "retiring" ceremony. Unless there is a party . . . in which case, he goes to bed at dawn!

* "Long live the king!" in French.

We followed the crowd through many richly frescoed rooms, and finally reached the king's bedroom.

A majestic rodent was seated on a canopy bed with embroidered drapes, wearing an enormouse curly wig. His brown eyes sparkled, and his snout showed signs of the smallpox he'd had as a mouselet. He wore a linen nightshirt, decorated with lace and fine EMBROIDERY.

A servant picked up his fancy golden chamber pot and gave it to me. "Empty that in the courtyard!"

I made a **face** and protested, "But why me?"

He replied, "It is an honor to serve the king!"

RISE AND SHINE!
The King was awakened at eight by the Valet de Chambre. A footman allowed in only those with the right to enter the king's chamber while the officers of the Wardrobe and Chamber ensured that the king was washed, shaved, combed, and given his breakfast.

The courtiers all began to shout, "Me! Let me! I want to empty the king's **chamber pot**!"

Holey cheese, they would do anything to impress the king!

Grumbling, I trotted down the stairs, emptied the chamber pot, and hurried back to the king's room. Yuck!

One page put an embroidered **shirt** on the king, another one tied his **shoes**, and a third handed him his **SWORD**.

The king ate breakfast on his bed, leaning against some **soft** lace pillows. Then we followed him to a different room, where he took a seat on his throne.

All of the courtiers bowed to the king and asked him for **favors**, help, and ADVICE. Many wished him an early happy birthday. (His birthday was the next day, September 5!)

The king answered everyone's requests cautiously. "*Je verrai . . .* * "

When it was our turn, we bowed before him. The king yawned. "**What a bore!**"

Trap shrugged. "Your Majesty, I have an idea. If you're bored, you should throw a PARTY for your birthday."

The king exclaimed, "What a fabumouse idea! Well done, *monsieur*!"

All around us, the courtiers WHISPERED excitedly . . .

Pssst . . . what a great idea . . . what a great idea . . .

* I will see.

A PARTY WORTHY OF THE SUN KING . . . OR ELSE!

The king thought for a moment. "But who will organize this **PARTY** for me?"

Without hesitating, Trap pointed at me. "My cousin Gerôme can do it! He's a party-planning specialist!"

Your Majesty, we pay you our respects!

My whiskers wobbled and my tail twitched. "Um, I —"

The king **thundered**, "You will organize a party for me! It must be a party that lasts all day and all night, a party truly worthy of a king, or else . . . THWACK!"

All of the courtiers murmured. "Pssst . . . otherwise . . . otherwise . . . otherwise . . . THWACK! The king will cut off his head . . . THWACK!"

An enormouse executioner standing nearby began to sharpen the BLADE of his ax. He boomed, "Who do I need to decapitate? I'm ready!"

The Grand Chamberlain, François LeFraud, snickered **wickedly**. "No one — for now!"

Squeak! What trouble had Trap gotten me into now? When the king left, I turned to the crowd of courtiers. "Um, can you kind rodents help us

organize the PARTY?"

They were all **silent**.

Trap turned to one nearby courtier. "*Monsieur,** can you help us organize the PARTY?"

The mouse scurried away, muttering, "OOOOH, I'm so sorry, but I need to go get my fur trimmed!"

Trap turned to a blond mouse. "*Madame,*** could you —"

She slipped away before he could finish his

We have to do it alone!

I must go! Me, too! Me, too!

* Sir   ** Madam

question. "OOOOH, the dressmaker is waiting for me!"

A snooty female rodent in a lace dress hissed, "OOOOH, no one will help you! They're all **jealous** because the king took an interest in you. So they all want your party to be a complete failure!"

We were stunned. Holey cheese! "Really?"

The mouse turned and ran away with an excuse

Me, too! Me, too! Me, too! Otherwise . . . thwack!

of her own. "You **FOOLS**! It's clear that you aren't used to the courtly life. But I can't **HELP** you, either. Um, I must go to the . . . paw doctor!"

I spun around to face my cousin, **red** in the snout with anger. "Why did you say that I would organize the party?!"

Trap scoffed, "Oh, come on, Gerrykins. What do you need to organize the king's **BIRTHDAY** party? Some lanterns, a few placecards, a little *cake* with some candles . . ."

"But how many people will be invited?" I yelled.

Trap shrugged. "Well, probably about a ***thousand***? One thousand, two thousand, three thousand? Who knows?"

I squeaked in desperation. "WHAAAAAAAT?!" Then I sobbed. "I'll never be able to organize a party for more than a thousand rodents. The Sun King will cut off my head! *THWACK!*"

Thea put an arm around my shoulders.

"Come on, big brother, cheer up. I'll handle the decorations."

Benjamin squeezed my paw. "I'll be your assistant!"

Even Trap piped up. "And I'll take care of the food, of course. I'll start making a list of everything I need!"

Just then, we heard a cry coming from the queen's apartments. "Thief! Someone stole my Royal Medallion!"

So, I need this . . . and that . . . plus, this . . .

Wait — this list is enormouse!

WHO STOLE THE ROYAL MEDALLION?

We ran to the queen's apartments, which were also on the second floor.

Two mice were restraining a **frightened** young blond mouse. They were taking orders from a rodent with reddish fur and a curly black wig.

The rodent in charge wore an emerald-colored outfit with lace trim and **ruby** buttons. His long, muddy shoes had square heels and were

She did it!

decorated with green silk bows. His right ankle was bandaged. I knew this mouse — it was the chamberlain we had seen before, François LeFraud!

LeFraud YELLED furiously, "She did it! She stole the Royal Medallion!"

At that moment, a lady rodent with a kind snout walked in. She wore a beautiful blue silk dress. Holey cheese, it was the queen, Marie-Thérèse!

While the ladies and gentlemice gossiped, the queen peered at the **sad** mouse being held by the butlers.

"Corrine! Did you really steal the Royal Medallion and my jewelry box? You know the king gave me that locket as a reminder of our wedding."

The mouse threw herself at the queen's feet,

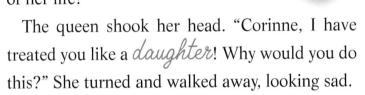

sobbing. "*Ma reine*,* I am **innocent**!"

LeFraud sneered. "You say you're innocent, but the medallion is gone. Call the **Musketeers** — they will put her in prison for the rest of her life!"

The queen shook her head. "Corinne, I have treated you like a *daughter*! Why would you do this?" She turned and walked away, looking sad.

I knew it was the Musketeers' duty to protect the royal family. I had to do something before they arrived! So I stepped up and introduced myself to the chamberlain. "My name is *Stiltoneaux, Gerôme Stiltoneaux*. Before she is condemned, this young lady has the right to a standard trial!"

LeFraud laughed **evilly**. "What right? What

* My queen

trial? We condemn her, and that's it!"

I insisted, "What PROOF do you have that she is guilty?"

He scowled at me. "First of all, Corinne is the queen's chambermaid — she had plenty of chances to poke around in her bedroom. Plus, she is PENNILESS. Of course she wanted to make her life better by selling the medallion. But instead, she will spend her life in prison!" He gave a wicked laugh.

We don't have time . . . Otherwise . . . thwack!

Corinne threw herself at my paws. "*Monsieur*, help me! I would never do any harm to the queen. She has always been so good to me! I swear — I am poor, that's true, but I'm an honest mouse!"

She stared into my eyes. I knew that she was telling the truth!

Thea whispered sadly, "Geronimo,

we don't have TIME to help her. We need to hurry and organize the king's party — otherwise . . ."

We have to save her!

Trap moved a finger across his throat. "Otherwise . . . THWACK!"

But Benjamin tugged at my jacket. "Uncle, we have to save her!"

I thought and thought and thought and thought and thought and thought and thought and thought and thought . . .

WE NEEDED TO HELP THAT INNOCENT MOUSE!

So I squeaked, "Corinne, I will save you!"

I will save you!

A MYSTERIOUS CASE

Before I could do anything else, a confident cavalier entered the room. He had elegant curly whiskers, and was wearing a red tunic and feathered hat. It was Carlo Camembert, the head of the queen's Musketeers!

He was about to carry Corinne away, but I cried, "Give me one hour! I will prove her **innocence**!"

LeFraud **YELLED**, "Don't listen to him!"

Camembert turned to look at me. "Why are you defending this young mouse?"

I stood up tall and responded, "For the love of *justice*!"

Camembert smoothed his whiskers. "So be it, sir! Musketeer's honor, I give you one hour to prove this young mouse's innocence — but no more!"

It was already six o'clock in the **EVENING**. We needed to solve this **mysterious** case in two shakes of a rat's tail!

I immediately left to inspect the royal apartments for **CLUES**.

THE MUSKETEERS

This was a group of armed soldiers, whose main duty was to protect the royal family (almost like bodyguards). They were trained in using muskets, advanced weaponry for the time. That's how they got their name!

The adventures of the Musketeers were fictionalized by Alexandre Dumas in his well-known novel, *The Three Musketeers*, written in 1844.

① I examined the queen's room.

I noticed that a green silk bow had gotten caught in a vase of roses.

Conclusion: Someone had lost a green bow!

? ? ? ? ? ? ? ? ? ? ? ? ? ? ? ? ?

I remembered that I had seen a green bow somewhere . . . but when?

FIRST CLUE!

A green silk bow!

② I opened the window.

I noticed that there was both a tuft of **reddish fur** and a **curly black hair** on the windowsill.

Conclusion: Someone had entered through the window!

? ? ? ? ? ? ? ? ? ? ? ? ? ? ? ? ? ? ?

I remembered that I had seen someone with reddish fur and black hair . . . but where?

SECOND CLUE!

A tuft of reddish fur!

And a curly black hair!

(3) I looked out the window.

I noticed that it had rained. The ground was damp! Down in the garden, there were suspicious **SHOE PRINTS**.

Conclusion: Someone had climbed up to the queen's window from the garden!

? ? ? ? ? ? ? ? ? ? ? ? ? ? ? ? ? ? ? ?

I remembered that I had seen someone with muddy shoes . . . but why?

THIRD CLUE!

Shoe prints in the garden!

④ I went to the garden and studied the prints.

The thief was wearing a big shoe with a square heel! The prints that led away from the palace were **DEEPER** than the prints that led toward the palace — especially on the left foot.

Conclusion: The thief had a limp, and left with the heavy jewelry box and medallion!

? ? ? ? ? ? ? ? ? ? ? ? ? ? ? ? ? ?

I remembered that I had seen someone with square-heeled shoes, long feet, and a limp . . . but who?

FOURTH CLUE!

What strange prints!

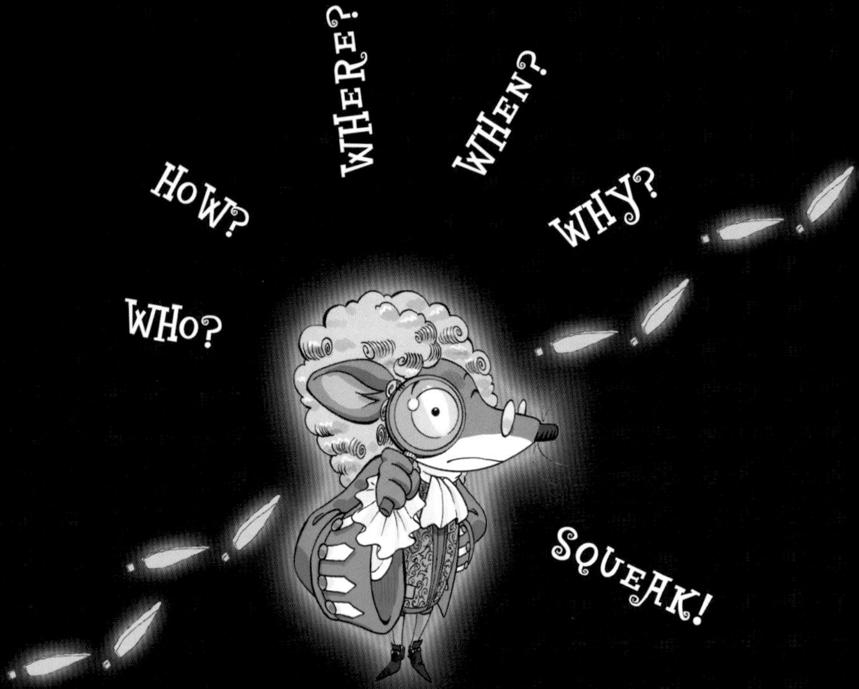
WHO?
HOW?
WHERE?
WHEN?
WHY?
SQUEAK!

VERY STRANGE!

I called my family over and showed them what I'd found. "Let's **follow** the prints!"

Together, we left the **palace** . . . turned right . . . crossed the Parterre du Nord . . . passed the *Pyramid Fountain* . . . and arrived at the Water Walk.

The shoe prints stopped right in front of the DRAGON FOUNTAIN!

At the center of the fountain was a dragon, surrounded by tiny **cherubs** with bows and arrows, riding on swans.

VERY STRANGE! There was no water coming out of the dragon's mouth — but why?

What a mystery!

Just then, I got an **idea**. Without stopping to think about it, I jumped into the fountain and

Quick . . .

. . . let's follow . . .

. . . the . . .

. . . tracks!

We turned right . . . crossed the North Terrace . . . passed the Pyramid Fountain . . . arrived at the

DRAGON FOUNTAIN

PALACE

Water Walk . . . and the footprints stopped in front of the Dragon Fountain!

climbed the fierce dragon statue!

I looked in the dragon's mouth . . . and saw the jewelry box!

"**Thundering cat tails – I found it!**" I cried.

I pulled out the jewelry box. Immediately, a stream of water poured out of the dragon's mouth again.

With my family looking on, I opened the jewelry box. The **Royal Medallion** was inside!

The dragon's mouth

WE HAVE CRACKED THE CASE!

We ran back to the **palace** just as the palace clock struck seven. We had found the precious Royal Medallion, and I had figured out who **stole** it!

I announced to the court, "One hour has passed, and we have cracked the case!"

The long and splendid HALL OF MIRRORS filled with courtiers. Camembert arrived, then the queen, and finally the king.

I began my speech. "Beautiful ladies and valiant gentlemice, we have gathered here to solve this **mysterious** case!"

I began to explain everything that I had discovered.

★ THE MYSTERY OF THE ★ ROYAL MEDALLION

1. In the queen's room, I noticed a green lace bow . . .

   ★ Grand Chamberlain LeFraud was wearing shoes with green bows!

2. Near the queen's window, I noticed a tuft of reddish fur, and a piece of curly black hair . . .

   ★ Grand Chamberlain LeFraud had reddish fur and wore a curly black wig!

★ ★ ★ ★ ★

★ ★ ★ ★ ★ ★ ★ ★ ★

③ **In the garden, I noticed shoe prints on the wet ground . . .**

⭐ Grand Chamberlain LeFraud's shoes were muddy!

④ **The prints were long, had square heels, and belonged to someone who limped and carried the heavy jewelry box with the medallion inside.**

⭐ Grand Chamberlain LeFraud wore long shoes with square heels and limped on his right foot — so he left with the jewelry box!

★ ★ ★ ★ ★ ★ ★ ★

CONCLUSION: Grand Chamberlain LeFraud was guilty!

WHO IS GUILTY?

 As I finished my explanation, I noticed that *LeFraud* was trying to slip out the door!

Thea grabbed him by the tail. "Oh, no, you sneaky rat — now **you're** the one going to prison!"

He hollered in panic, "I didn't do it! I didn't hide the jewelry box in the **dragon's mouth**!"

I smiled under my whiskers. "Interesting! I didn't say where I found the jewelry box. How did you know where it was **hidden**, LeFraud, if you didn't **steal** it? You just gave us even more proof that you're guilty!"

The scoundrel's fur turned even redder. "What a **FOOL** — I gave myself away!" he mumbled.

Then he cried, "Fine! But do you know why I stole the Royal Medallion? To get Corinne in TROUBLE!" He paused and looked down at the floor. "I wanted to marry her, but she fell in love with a farmer from her village. I was heartbroken. So I decided to get back at her — and I would have succeeded if you hadn't arrived, *Stiltoneaux*, you worthless rodent!"

With that, Camembert ordered, "Musketeers, take him away!"

I bowed to the **queen**. "And now, Your Majesty, let me return your medallion!"

I handed over the jewelry box. The queen lifted the lid and smiled as she pulled out the Royal Medallion. It sparkled like a star!

The queen opened the medallion and kissed the small painting of the king inside. Then she put it around her neck.

"Thank you, dear *Stiltoneaux*. I'm thrilled that Corinne is innocent! As a reward, I will anoint you and your companions all MUSKETEERS."

The Musketeers all cried in unison, "All for one, and one for all!"

Pssst . . . the jewelry box . . . the jewelry box . . .

They carried us out in triumph.

Corinne ran up and hugged me, tears rolling down her snout. "Monsieur Stiltoneaux, you SAVED me!" She paused, looking worried. "But how will you organize a party for the KING now?"

The sun was setting. It was late already!

I sighed. "There's no time to organize the king's party by tomorrow morning."

Trap grumbled grimly, "Oh yeah, no big deal. They'll just chop off our heads. THWACK!"

Corinne looked DESPERATE. "I don't want anything bad to happen to you because of me!" With a wave over her shoulder, she SCURRIED

Pssst . . . the jewelry box . . . the jewelry box . . .

away. "I have an idea. I'll be right back!"

For the love of cheese — where was she going?

Hours went by, and we sat in the **gardens**, halfheartedly trying to plan some sort of party. Trap sadly read the looooong list of materials we needed.

"We need cheeses, fruits, vegetables,

meat, **FISH** . . . without quality ingredients, not even a great chef like me can create a magnificent banquet!"

Suddenly, I saw many SHADOWS silently advancing in the dark.

My fur stood on end, and I squeaked in fear. "Who's there?"

THAT'S WHAT
FRIENDS ARE FOR!

I heard a voice in the **dark**. "Don't worry, Monsieur Stiltoneaux, it's us!"

"Us who?" I asked hesitantly.

The reply made me sigh with relief. "It's Corinne and all my friends — the farmers and **peasants** from the nearby village!"

A friendly looking young mouse named Pierre squeezed my paw. "Thank you for saving my **fiancée**!"

I smiled. "That's what friends are for!"

Corinne and Pierre

"Since you saved Corinne," Pierre said, "we'll help you organize the **PARTY** for the king by tomorrow morning!"

Thea, Trap, and Benjamin all turned to me and **cheered**. "We can do it!"

I grabbed our list.

"Here's how we'll organize everything! We'll work all night, in three **teams**. The **FIRST**, led by Thea, will put up decorations. The **SECOND** team, led by me, will move the tables and chairs, and set the tables. Benjamin will be my assistant. The **THIRD** team, led by Trap, will cook!"

> **FRIENDSHIP**
>
> It's nice to help our friends! A true friend understands when you're sad and when you're happy. Good friends know what you need and offer to help you before you even ask! Friends understand each other, without having to say a word. No matter if they live near or far, friends are always close in our hearts.

Trap sniffed, "Okay, but what will we cook?"

Corinne smiled. *"Voilà!** We brought carts filled with **meat**, **FISH**, vegetables, **fruit**, **MILK**, **butter**, cheeses, **flour**, and **eggs** — anything you could possibly need to prepare a banquet fit for a king."

What a mouserific relief!

---

* Here!

We got to work right away. As we worked, Corinne told me what village life was like.

Listening to Corinne's stories, I couldn't help thinking that there was a big difference between the way that the **gentlemice** lived and the way the farmers lived during the Sun King's reign. **It just didn't seem right!**

What do we need for the party?

Meat	**Fish**	**Vegetables**
Fruit	**Milk**	**Flour**
Cheese	**Grains**	**Eggs**

How the Nobles Lived

The noble ladies and gentlemen during the reign of the Sun King lived in luxury. Much attention was paid to the latest fashions, including clothing, wigs, accessories, and jewelry. The main duty of the nobles at Versailles was to attend to the king, and they were often very busy at parties, plays, ballets, operas, and gambling nights thrown by Louis XIV himself.

It's your turn, Duke!

How elegant!

Thank you, Count!

Nice cards!

A group of noblemice playing cards

How the Farmers Lived

The farmers often tended to fields owned by the noblemen. They worked hard in frequently difficult conditions! Food was scarce, taxes were high, and bad harvests led to famine. Because of poor hygiene and hard living conditions, French farmers and peasants often got sick.

How did the harvest go?

It was good...

...but our taxes went up again!

Sigh!

A group of farmers go to the market

THREE TRAGEDIES!

While Trap was busy cooking, I heard him scream. **"Aaaaaagh!"**

I ran to him, worried. "What's wrong?"

"It's a **tragedy**!" he cried dramatically.

I turned white. "What happened? Can I help?"

He pointed to the palace in the distance. "I forgot the salt! What would the king say? Someone — like you — needs go get it right away!"

I sighed. "Oh, all right. I'll go get you the salt."

Salt

I set out as *FAST* as my paws would carry me. Whew — the road back to the palace was so **loooooong**!

I finally arrived at the palace kitchens, grabbed the salt, and turned back around.

When I arrived, Trap yelled, "There's been a second tragedy! I also forgot the **pepper**! What would the king say? Someone — like you — needs to go get it right away!"

Pepper

I rolled my eyes. "Um, is that really necessary?"

"*Oui!**"

Once again, I trudged down the long road that ran between the palace and the garden where the party was being held. I arrived in the kitchens, grabbed the **P E P P E R**, and turned back around.

Mustard

When I arrived, Trap yelled, "There's been a third tragedy! I forgot the mustard! What would the king say? Someone — like you — needs to go get it right away!"

My fur stood on end.

"*Non!*** That's enough!"

* Yes!   ** No!

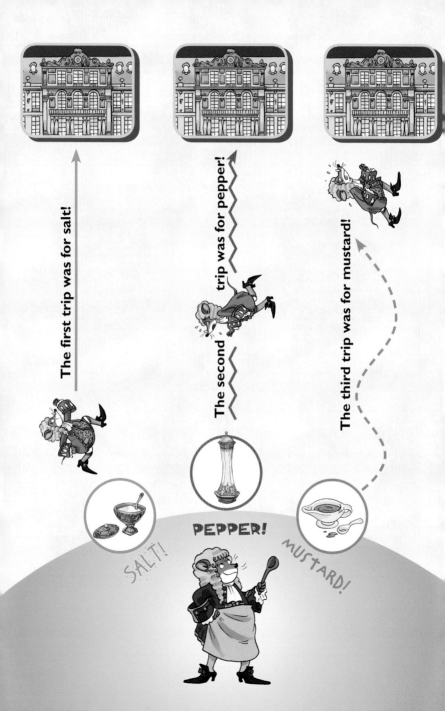

The first trip was for salt!

The second trip was for pepper!

The third trip was for mustard!

SALT!

PEPPER!

MUSTARD!

Then Trap begged, *"S'il te plait . . .*"*

I'm such a softy! So of course, I ran to find the mustard.

But when I returned this time, I was completely **exhausted**. My tongue was hanging out, and I was out of breath!

Trap thanked me. *"Merci!**"*

I grunted, "One more step, and I think I would have **collapsed**!"

Poor Uncle!

Huff! Puff!

ROSE PETALS AND SILVER TRUMPETS

The next morning, the musicians played a **HAPPY** tune while the party guests began to arrive at the palace. I could hardly believe it, but the Party was under way!

Trap walked around the tables, giving out his **FINAL ORDERS**. "Thea, slice another cake. Benjamin, bring that vase of roses over here. Geronimo, move those glasses to this table. No, not that one — this one! Hmph, why do I always have to do everything?"

Soon, the **KING** and queen arrived in a golden carriage. It was drawn by white horses

with **RED** silk bows tied in their thick manes!

The king wore a red silk outfit with lace ribbon trim, and his pearl embroidered cloak *waved* in the wind. His golden spurs sparkled, and the feathers on his ornate hat flapped in the wind. The king's attendants spread rose petals in his path, and silver trumpets *blared*.

The Royal Poet announced, "The **KING** has arrived! He is punctual, like May roses, like the sun at dawn, like . . ."

Trap snickered. "Yeah, punctual like a stomachache after eating too much, like a toothache when you have a cavity, like . . ."

I turned WHITE. "Be quiet, or they'll cut off our heads! THWACK!"

Trap bowed before the king and gave him a canapé. *"Bon appétit!*"*

The king took a bite and licked his whiskers. *"Délicieux!**"*

* Enjoy your meal!   ** Delicious!

Have you heard?

Who cares?

A mouse named *Madame Gossipez* opened a fan right in front of my snout. "**OOOOOOH**, have you heard the latest juicy court gossip? The brother of the doorman of the paw doctor of the hairdresser of the valet of the butler of the uncle of the royal hairdresser told me that the king has an ugly **wart** on the tip of his tail! But don't tell anyone — it's a secret!"

Trap **SHRUGGED**. "Humph. Who cares?"

After a long time, I was finally able to **escape** from the gossiping rodent.

But at that moment,

STRANGE REMEDIES!
Doctors during the time of the Sun King had some strange ideas. They believed that washing with water could be bad for your health, and they often cured diseases by bloodletting (putting leeches on the skin to suck the patient's blood)!

the **ROYAL** doctor approached me. He began to suggest a bunch of strange remedies!

"*Stiltoneaux,* you're awfully $PALE$! How do you feel?"

"Good, thanks."

"Are you sure? You don't look so good! Can I do anything to help you?"

"I'm fine, thanks."

"How about a nice bloodletting with some $LEECHES$?"

I ran away as fast as my paws would take me. "No, no, no, thank you! I am really quite fine!"

Can I help you? How about a nice bloodletting?

PARTIES

Parties during the reign of the Sun King involved everything from gambling nights, to feasts, to ballet performances, to operas, to fireworks. There were elaborate banquets, and the mood was lightened by the music of composer Jean-Baptiste Lully. Molière's comedies were often performed, along with Jean Racine's tragedies.

The **party** went wonderfully, and finally the most anticipated moment of the evening arrived — **the Great Dance**!

The king smiled and held a paw out to Thea. *"Ma chérie, voulez-vous danser avec moi?**"*

My dear mouse, would you like to dance with me?

* My dear mouse, would you like to dance with me?

All of the ladies of the court whispered, "Ooooooooh, we're so jealous!"

The **birthday party** lasted all day and night, and ended with magnificent fireworks. Trap looked around and said thoughtfully, "All of these noble rodents **eat and eat and eat**. But who pays for it all?"

Thea sighed. "The French people! The **KING** and the members of the government tax the workers too much. In about one hundred years, at the time of **LOUIS XVI** and **Marie Antoinette**, this sort of thing will all lead to the **FRENCH REVOLUTION**!"

The tri-colored flag that was born from the French Revolution — now the official flag of France!

I Am the Sun King!

Dawn was already breaking. My family and I lay on the dewy grass and looked up at the **PINK** sky. Versailles sparkled in the sun's first rays.

Trap grinned. "We've had a lot of **fun** here, don't you think, Cousin?"

I muttered, "Yeah, almost as much fun as that time I **slammed** my paw in a door." But I had to smile. It had certainly been an adventure!

Benjamin squeaked, "I'm happy we saved Corinne."

Thea added, dreamily, "I **danced** with a real king. What an unforgettable party!"

A voice behind us said, "It truly was an **unforgettable** party!"

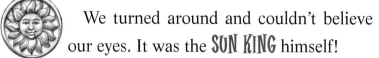

We turned around and couldn't believe our eyes. It was the SUN KING himself!

The king greeted us with a wave of his feathery cap. Then he continued, "To organize a party like that truly takes a special group of mice — like you!"

I bowed
    until
        my whiskers
           grazed
                the ground.

"Your Majesty, we are honored," I said. "Now, may I ask you . . ."

A wave of sadness passed over the king's face. "Go ahead. Everyone asks the king for something. What would you like?"

I smiled. "Your Majesty, I really just wanted to ask if you had a **good time** at the party. That's all."

He was stunned. "You don't want anything from

me? I can give you HONOR, MONEY, or POWER with a snap of my fingers. I am the SUN KING!"

I smiled. "Your Majesty, you don't find happiness in the things you have, but in the rodent you are! And in FRIENDSHIP, like we now have with the mice from Corinne's village who helped us arrange your party."

The king looked thoughtful. "I like the way you think, Stiltoneaux. Here in the COURT, they only seem to care about clothing, jewelry, and gossip! Maybe we can learn something from the villagers."

I checked the time. Moldy mozzarella, we had to get out of there! "Your Majesty, I'm so sorry, but we need to go."

The king seemed disappointed. "You're leaving? Just as we were becoming friends?"

I asked his forgiveness. "I don't want to seem rude, but we have a long JOURNEY ahead of us."

The Sun King insisted, "But I need rodents like you at my side! I will make you a **count**! No, a **marquis**! No, no, a **DUKE**!"

I bowed before him. "Your Majesty, we must go, but I hope we'll see you again someday. *Adieu!**"

He smiled and shook my paw. "I hope so, too. *Bon voyage!***"

Bon voyage!

Adieu!

* Farewell!   ** Have a safe trip!

With that, my family and I dashed back to the rosebush where we had hidden **THE RODENT RELOCATOR**, and changed into our **orange** jumpsuits. I was so happy to be rid of those flea-ridden clothes!

Now

    we

        were

           ready

               to

                  return

                     home!

I TOLD YOU NOT TO PRESS IT!

We entered all of the information for our trip home, and THE RODENT RELOCATOR began to spin and spin and spin . . .

I was just wondering why the professor had told us never to touch the **RED BUTTON**, when suddenly Trap yelled, "Uh, guys, I need to tell you something!"

"What?" I cried.

He shouted, "Um, I . . ."

"You what?"

"I *TOUCHED* . . ."

"You **TOUCHED** what?"

A horrible thought ran through my head.

I WHISPERED, "Y-you

didn't by chance touch . . . the **RED BUTTON**?!"

The Professor told us to never press the red button!

Trap put his snout in his paws. "Yes! I touched it!"

I tugged on my whiskers in desperation. "Why would you do that?!"

A computerized voice began to count backward over the speaker. *"TEN . . . NINE . . . EIGHT . . ."*

I was starting to tie my tail in knots. "**EIGHT? EIGHT** seconds until what? I want to know! No, maybe I don't want to know! What are we going to do? Heeeeeelp!"

Thea raised her eyebrows. "There's no point in yelling! No one else is going to hear you."

Meanwhile, the voice continued its countdown. *"SEVEN . . . SIX . . . FIVE . . . FOUR . . . THREE . . . TWO . . . ONE . . ."*

I heard a strange noise . . .

As the Rodent Relocator was spinning . . .
You touched what?
1
2
You touched the what?!
You didn't touch the red button, did you?!
3
4
A terrible thought ran through my head!

BING!

I squeaked, "Heeeeeelp! What's happening?"

1 Five cheesy toasts popped out of a toaster oven!

2 A bright light went on!

3 A stereo began playing deafening music!

4 A camera flashed!

5 A video camera began recording!

6 A table popped up with five glasses on it!

7 A cheese smoothie appeared!

SO THAT'S WHAT THE RED BUTTON WAS FOR!

THE RODENT RELOCATOR stopped abruptly. After all that chaos, we were totally dazed. That had been a fur-raising ride! We climbed out with our snouts spinning and spinning and spinning and spinning and spinning and spinning and spinning and spinning and spinning and spinning!

Squeak!

But we

were happy,

because it looked

like we were

home!

And what's better than returning home after a long journey?

Professor von Volt appeared, smiling and holding his paws out in welcome. "Oh, you figured out what the **RED BUTTON** was for!"

With my head still spinning, I mumbled, "Not exactly! What *is* it for, Professor?"

He grinned. "To **celebrate** your return! That's why I said you should never press it **during** the trip!"

Slimy Swiss cheese, what a relief!

As quick as a wink, Trap shoved a cheesy toast into his mouth. "**Yum** — let's **celebrate**!"

As we enjoyed our welcome-home feast, Volt asked me, "So, how did your **JOURNEY THROUGH TIME** go?"

"It was another **FABUMOUSE** adventure, Professor! I'm only sorry about one thing: When I was in Chichén Itzá, I almost got my paws on some precious **Maya books** . . ."

Volt turned **PALE**. "Geronimo — are you telling me that you tried to save the Maya books?"

Dejected, I nodded. "Yes."

Volt stammered, "And did you *SUCCEED*?"

I sighed. "Unfortunately, no."

Volt **LEAPED UP** in happiness. "Oh, thank goodmouse!" Then he explained, "If something gets changed when you go back in **time**, you run the **RISK** of changing history forever! For example, if you went back in time and you stopped my parents from getting **married**, I wouldn't exist anymore! You should **never** interrupt the space-time continuum!"

THE SPACE-TIME CONTINUUM

According to Albert Einstein, the universe has three dimensions in space — left/right, up/down, and forward/backward — and one dimension in time. This four-dimensional space is called the space-time continuum. In science fiction, this means that if you change something in a previous time, it creates consequences in the future.

Professor von Volt's parents were married and had a child
(Professor von Volt).

If his parents had **NOT** gotten married, they would **NOT** have
had a child, and Professor von Volt would no longer exist!

BENJAMIN'S CLASS

The professor's explanation was so interesting that Benjamin asked, "Professor von Volt, could you come to my classroom and talk about time?"

The professor agreed, so the next day, we all went to SCHOOL with Benjamin. His classmates asked about a million questions!

Oliver, Benjamin's friend who loves SCIENCE, asked Volt, "Professor, what is the space-time continuum?"

I'm Oliver!

After Volt had answered Oliver's question and many others, Benjamin's teacher announced, "Okay, class.

Benjamin's teacher

Let's all **thank** the professor for coming to speak with us! Now it's time to move on to history. Benjamin, is your research on daily life in **ancient Rome** ready?"

Benjamin squeaked, "Of course!" While we watched from the back of the classroom, he began to talk **enthusiastically** about the streets, the houses, the food, and the clothing in ancient Rome.

When he finished, his teacher looked awfully **impressed**. "Cheese and crackers, what interesting research!"

Benjamin's friend Bugsy Wugsy, who loves learning about history, gave him a high five.

I was happy for my nephew. "We need to **celebrate** — and I have a mouserific idea! Let's throw a historical costume party at *The Rodent's Gazette*!"

I'm Bugsy Wugsy!

A COSTUME PARTY!

The next day, many **STRANGE** characters showed up at *The Rodent's Gazette*: Cleopatra, the queen of Egypt; two knights in armor; a pirate; an ancient Roman citizen in a chariot; a mummy; a dinosaur . . .

They were all Benjamin's **FRIENDS**, in costume!

Guess who dressed up as **Napoléon Bonaparte**? My grandfather, William Shortpaws, naturally! **Festive** music was playing, and many mice began to dance.

Trap jabbed me with his elbow. "Hey, Cousin, why don't you show everyone a real **Maya dance**?"

I blushed. "Um, actually, I'm not feeling very inspired today!"

Trap grinned. "Oh, you need inspiration now, huh? Maybe because there are no toucan SURPRISES here at *The Rodent's Gazette*?"

He laughed — and so did I. I was too happy to be annoyed at his jokes this time!

I sat down and nibbled on a morsel of cheese, thinking about our amazing journey. I couldn't believe everything we'd seen, the mice we'd met, and the incredible history we'd uncovered! The biggest thing I'd learned was that we're all a **PART** of history. Everything we do, no matter how small, can change the course of history forever. I had so much to write about now! It had been wonderful to learn about different times and places by seeing them up close.

As I thought over the last few days, I couldn't help saying to myself,

"*We are history!*"

WHERE? WHERE? WHERE?

After the party, I was about to leave *The Rodent's Gazette* office when Professor von Volt whispered, "Geronimo, let me tell you a secret — maybe someday you'll go on another JOURNEY THROUGH TIME!"

Benjamin, who overheard us, squeaked, "Where?"

Thea added impatiently, "Where? Where?"

Trap shouted, "Where? Where? Where?"

Volt laughed. "Who knows where? Maybe you'll travel to the time of the MAMMOTHS, or to ANCIENT GREECE, or to early AMERICA, or maybe to the period when LEONARDO DA VINCI was alive. Who knows?"

who knows?

Volt smoothed his whiskers. "After all, you've already proven that you can certainly handle a fabumouse, marvelous, ambitious, adventurous, hilarious, audacious, vigorous, courageous, **CURIOUS**, joyous, GLORIOUS, victorious, mysterious, torturous trip!"

We shouted in unison:

"Hooray for traveling through time!"

I hope you liked my latest adventure, and I hope that this JOURNEY THROUGH TIME inspired you to be passionate about history and curious to know more. Everything that has happened in the past helps us better understand who we are now — and what will happen next!

Dear rodent friends,
My second journey through
time was extraordinary!
To keep track of what we
discovered during this
adventure, I've prepared
a special travel journal
for you, full of games and
activities.

Let's have fun together!

Geronimo Stilton

Ancient Rome

MAKE YOUR OWN ROMAN MOSAIC!

I Draw a crescent moon and cloud on the white posterboard.

II Measure one-inch marks all along the edges of the colored paper (both lengthwise and widthwise). With the pencil, draw lines at these intervals to make lots of one-inch squares, as if you were making a chessboard.

III With the round-edged scissors, cut out the squares on each sheet of paper. These are the tiles for your mosaic!

IV Glue the red squares along the edges of the poster board to make a border.

V Fill in the background of the design by gluing down the blue and light blue squares — this is the sky!

VI Glue the yellow squares inside the moon, and the white ones inside the cloud.

Now you have a fabumouse Roman mosaic!

IMAGINE THAT YOU ARE WATCHING A CHARIOT RACE AT THE CIRCUS MAXIMUS.

ON A SEPARATE SHEET OF PAPER, WRITE AN ARTICLE ABOUT THE RACE! HERE ARE SOME QUESTIONS TO GET YOU THINKING LIKE AN ANCIENT SPORTS REPORTER:

What are the racers' names?

What is the atmosphere like at the race?

Who is in the lead at the first curve?

Who's in the lead at the second curve?

Do any racers crash or run off the track?

How do the racers try to beat one another?

Which chariot crosses the finish line first?

ROMAN NUMERALS

1 = I	6 = VI
2 = II	7 = VII
3 = III	8 = VIII
4 = IV	9 = IX
5 = V	10 = X

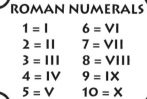

ROMAN GAMES

The people of ancient Rome played lots of fun games. You can try these yourself!

NUTS

Kids in ancient Rome played lots of fun games with nuts in the shell. They used them similar to the way kids today use marbles!

In one game, they placed three nuts on the ground, next to one another, so that they formed a small triangle. Then they placed a fourth nut on top, making a small pyramid shape. They challenged one another to throw another nut from a distance, attempting to knock over all the nuts at once!

MAKING DOLLS

Ancient Roman dolls were made of rag, wood, or bone, and some even had adjustable limbs. They often had clothes made of fabric. Try using a piece of fabric to make a toga for one of your favorite dolls or stuffed animals!

LEAPFROG & HIDE-AND-SEEK

Did you know that kids in ancient Rome are said to have played leapfrog and hide-and-seek, too? It may be hard to believe that those games that are played on playgrounds today have been around for thousands of years, but it's true!

WHAT DOESN'T BELONG?

Can you find the modern objects that don't belong in ancient Rome?

Answer: Potatoes, tomatoes, pineapples, and tea arrived in Europe only after the discovery of America, and ketchup is a modern recipe!

MAYA
CIVILIZATION

GROW A BEAN PLANT!

Beans were among the many crops that the Maya cultivated. Growing them is easy — you can try it yourself!

YOU NEED:
- 1 flowerpot saucer
- cotton balls
- 1 handful of fresh beans
- water

1. Cover the base of the flowerpot saucer with cotton balls.

2. Place the beans on top of the cotton balls, spreading them out so there's space between all of the beans.

3. Wet the beans, and put the flowerpot saucer in an area that gets a lot of light. Plants need water and light to grow! Remember to water the beans regularly.

4. After a few days, your beans will begin sprouting roots!

5 Watch the bean plants sprout! If you keep taking care of them, you will see them grow every day.

6 When the plants are about two inches tall, put them in a pot with some dirt, or plant them in a garden.

7 If you're patient, after a few months, beans will grow from your plant. Then you can ask your parents to cook them for you!

MAKE YOUR OWN JADE NECKLACE!

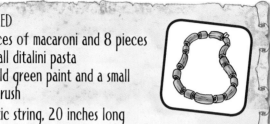

YOU NEED
- 8 pieces of macaroni and 8 pieces of small ditalini pasta
- emerald green paint and a small paintbrush
- 1 elastic string, 20 inches long

1 Using your paintbrush, paint the macaroni and ditalini with the green paint.

2 When the pasta is dry, thread the elastic through the pasta pieces. Alternate the macaroni and the ditalini one after the other.

3 Tie the ends of the string together and wear your pretty necklace — it will look similar to jade necklaces worn by the Maya!

MAYA ASTRONOMY

The ancient Maya carefully observed and recorded what happened in the sky above. They were avid astronomers! The planet Venus was very significant to the Maya. They associated it with war, and even planned battles to coincide with the movement of Venus through the sky.

Depending on the time of year, you'll be able to see Venus in the sky just before sunrise or just after sunset. As it travels around the sun inside the Earth's orbit, Venus spends about eight and a half months as a bright "morning star," then goes behind the sun and is not visible for about fifty days. Then Venus spends another eight and a half months as a bright "evening star," until it goes in front of the sun and is not visible for about eight days.

Look up there! It's Venus!

WHAT DOESN'T BELONG?

Can you find the modern objects that don't belong in the Maya village?

Answer: The watch, the soccer ball, the headphones, the metal cooking pot, and the CD player are all modern objects!

THE REIGN OF

THE SUN KING

THE VERSAILLES
GARDENS MAZE

Start here . . .

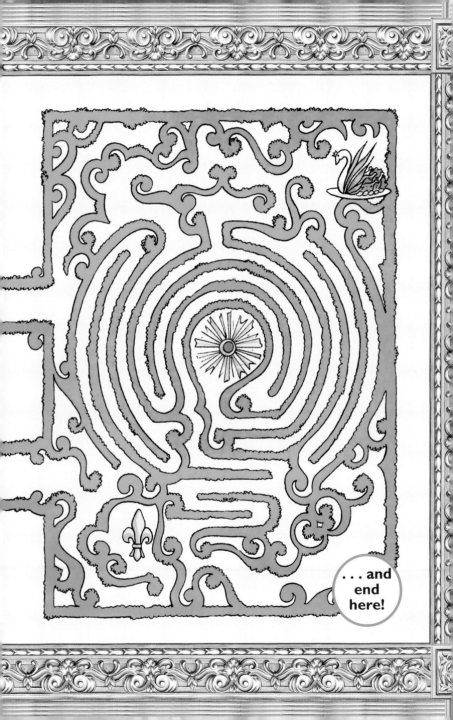

. . . and end here!

Imagine that you are the Sun King, and today is your birthday!

Try writing a short story about the big day, as if you lived in Versailles in 1682. Here are some ideas to get you started:

How would you prepare for the party?

What would you wear?

What kind of performances would there be?

What kinds of food would you have

at your banquet?

Who would be your lady or lordly love?

What presents would you get?

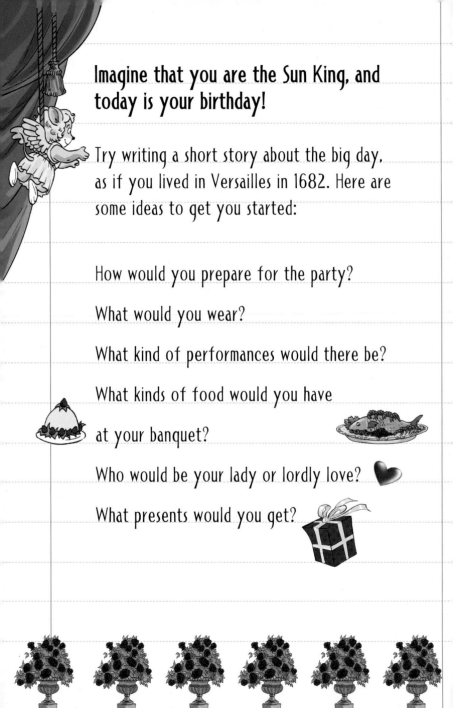

WHAT DOESN'T BELONG?

Can you find the modern objects that don't belong in the royal gardens?

Answer: The skateboard, the camera, the lawn mower, and the remote-control car are all modern objects!

Don't miss any of my other fabumouse adventures!

#1 Lost Treasure of the Emerald Eye

#2 The Curse of the Cheese Pyramid

#3 Cat and Mouse in a Haunted House

#4 I'm Too Fond of My Fur!

#5 Four Mice Deep in the Jungle

#6 Paws Off, Cheddarface!

#7 Red Pizzas for a Blue Count

#8 Attack of the Bandit Cats

#9 A Fabumouse Vacation for Geronimo

#10 All Because of a Cup of Coffee

#11 It's Halloween, You 'Fraidy Mouse!

#12 Merry Christmas, Geronimo!

#13 The Phantom of the Subway

#14 The Temple of the Ruby of Fire

#15 The Mona Mousa Code

#16 A Cheese-Colored Camper

#17 Watch Your Whiskers, Stilton!

#18 Shipwreck on the Pirate Islands

#19 My Name Is Stilton, Geronimo Stilton

#20 Surf's Up, Geronimo!

#21 The Wild, Wild West

#22 The Secret of Cacklefur Castle

A Christmas Tale

#23 Valentine's Day Disaster

#24 Field Trip to Niagara Falls

#25 The Search for Sunken Treasure

#26 The Mummy with No Name

#27 The Christmas Toy Factory

#28 Wedding Crasher

#29 Down and Out Down Under

#30 The Mouse Island Marathon

#31 The Mysterious Cheese Thief

Christmas Catastrophe

#32 Valley of the Giant Skeletons

#33 Geronimo and the Gold Medal Mystery

#34 Geronimo Stilton, Secret Agent

#35 A Very Merry Christmas

#36 Geronimo's Valentine

#37 The Race Across America

#38 A Fabumouse School Adventure

#39 Singing Sensation

#40 The Karate Mouse

#41 Mighty Mount Kilimanjaro

#42 The Peculiar Pumpkin Thief

#43 I'm Not a Supermouse!

#44 The Giant Diamond Robbery

#45 Save the White Whale!

#46 The Haunted Castle

#47 Run for the Hills, Geronimo!

#48 The Mystery in Venice

#49 The Way of the Samurai

#50 This Hotel Is Haunted!

#51 The Enormouse Pearl Heist

#52 Mouse in Space!

#53 Rumble in the Jungle

#54 Get into Gear, Stilton!

#55 The Golden Statue Plot

#56 Flight of the Red Bandit

The Hunt for the Golden Book

#57 The Stinky Cheese Vacation

#58 The Super Chef Contest

#59 Welcome to Moldy Manor

The Hunt for the Curious Cheese

#60 The Treasure of Easter Island

Don't miss my first journey through time!

Be sure to read all my adventures in the Kingdom of Fantasy!

THE KINGDOM OF FANTASY

THE QUEST FOR PARADISE:
THE RETURN TO THE KINGDOM OF FANTASY

THE AMAZING VOYAGE:
THE THIRD ADVENTURE IN THE KINGDOM OF FANTASY

THE DRAGON PROPHECY:
THE FOURTH ADVENTURE IN THE KINGDOM OF FANTASY

THE VOLCANO OF FIRE:
THE FIFTH ADVENTURE IN THE KINGDOM OF FANTASY

THE SEARCH FOR TREASURE:
THE SIXTH ADVENTURE IN THE KINGDOM OF FANTASY

THE ENCHANTED CHARMS:
THE SEVENTH ADVENTURE IN THE KINGDOM OF FANTASY

Don't miss these exciting Thea Sisters adventures!

Thea Stilton and the Dragon's Code

Thea Stilton and the Mountain of Fire

Thea Stilton and the Ghost of the Shipwreck

Thea Stilton and the Secret City

Thea Stilton and the Mystery in Paris

Thea Stilton and the Cherry Blossom Adventure

Thea Stilton and the Star Castaways

Thea Stilton: Big Trouble in the Big Apple

Thea Stilton and the Ice Treasure

Thea Stilton and the Secret of the Old Castle

Thea Stilton and the Blue Scarab Hunt

Thea Stilton and the Prince's Emerald

Thea Stilton and the Mystery on the Orient Express

Thea Stilton and the Dancing Shadows

Thea Stilton and the Legend of the Fire Flowers

Thea Stilton and the Spanish Dance Mission

Thea Stilton and the Journey to the Lion's Den

Thea Stilton and the Great Tulip Heist

Thea Stilton and the Chocolate Sabotage

Thea Stilton and the Missing Myth

Check out these very special editions featuring me and the Thea Sisters!

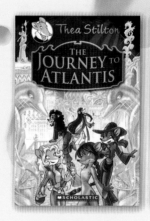

THE JOURNEY TO ATLANTIS

THE SECRET OF THE FAIRIES

THE SECRET OF THE SNOW

MEET GERONIMO STILTONIX

He is a spacemouse — the Geronimo Stilton of a parallel universe! He is captain of the spaceship *MouseStar 1*. While flying through the cosmos, he visits distant planets and meets crazy aliens. His adventures are out of this world!

#1 Alien Escape

#2 You're Mine, Captain!

#3 Ice Planet Adventure

#4 The Galactic Goal